MY FRIEND SAM

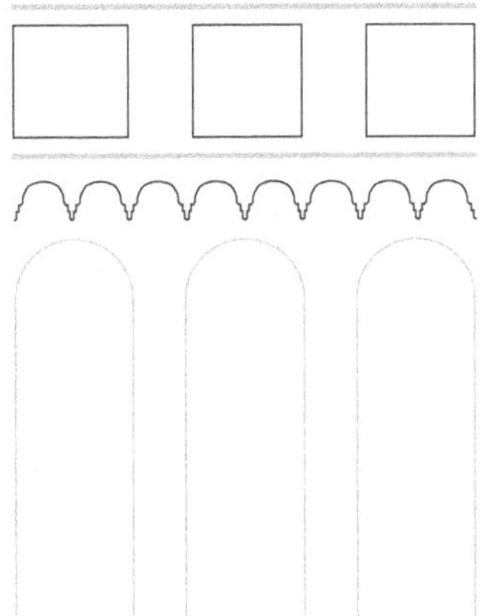

HENRY T. LARSEN

WRITE CREATIVE PRESS

www.writecreativepress.com

A catalogue record for this book is available from the National Library of Australia

It was on this side that my new power
tempted me until I fell in slavery.

Strange Case of Dr Jekyll and Mr Hyde

CONTENTS

« CHAPTER 1 »

Inspiration

Writers are vain, greedy and self-absorbed creatures. One learns three important lessons when dealing with these leeches. Firstly, don't give them any money. Secondly, never give them any power, and thirdly, and most importantly, never take anything they write seriously.

For one good line, a writer will destroy a friendship; for a paragraph, an entire family; and don't bother asking what they would do for a good book. Writers are immature, narcissistic, self-centred, stupid, politically daft, and cruel.

Take my good friend Sam, for instance.

I first met Sam in the year I set up my literary magazine, *Imagine*. The inspiration for *Imagine* came on my European sojourn while I gazed at the painting of *The Last Supper* at the Convent of Santa Mana della Grazie on a hot Milan afternoon in June. I don't know whether the crowds of sweaty flesh, or the sublime expression of each disciple caused it, but the ecstatic thought: *what this world needs is another literary magazine*, popped suddenly and unbidden into my head. I wanted to hug the bored-looking signorina attendant at the door. Instead, I gave her a tip of 300 euros, before strolling into the Mediterranean sun with my newfound vision.

All tour, this idea followed me like an affectionate dog as I wandered aimlessly from one significant artistic site to the next. As I meandered along the same paths Van Gogh no doubt traversed in Arles all those years ago, I realised I would either start my own magazine or be consumed with its latent energy. As I lifted my eyes to gaze upon Rodin's *The Thinker* in the Musée d'Orsay, I too contemplated the wonderful writers I would discover and launch upon the world. In the Hermitage Museum in St Petersburg, while gazing at Rembrandt's *Danaė*, I wondered whether I too could discover works of art as sublime as this.

Art can do this to a person. It can lift you up with the Gods — or as Sam said much later, it can cast you down with the devils.

I returned to Melbourne in the late Australian summer with my newfound vision and an indefatigable desire to turn the cultural wasteland of my homeland into a paradise of creativity: a poet on every corner, a masterpiece of art hanging from every spare wall.

I had nothing else to do with my life: my father having died only two years previously in a hang-gliding accident, and my dear mother dying in childbirth giving life to me. At twenty-nine, with no siblings or close relatives, except a maternal grandmother — and with a small fortune to my name, I set about realising my ecstatic European vision.

You've probably heard of my father, Doug Western, the founder of the Western Discount chain stores. You might remember his late-night TV ads from the 90s, with the cockatoo screeching: 'cheap, cheap prices'. Or the equally repeated ad of my father, with his sleeves rolled up, and his tie undone, pointing into the camera and saying: 'If you find a lower price at another store, we will give you the same item for free'.

The ad I remember best is not as famous as these. It's from the early 2000s. In this ad, my father sits at a desk with a blonde-haired, hazel-eyed boy on his lap. Surrounded by his staff, he stares into the camera and says: 'We know that in these tough times, families need good-quality products at low, low prices. Come in to one of our stores for a smile. At Westerns, we treat you like a family'. My father ends the ad by staring into the little boy's eyes and smiling.

I remember this ad so well, for I was the little boy, and anytime I'm feeling a little blue, I replay this ad on YouTube, re-living that one special moment of my life. I sat on his lap for ninety glorious minutes or 'eleven f***** takes', as Dad had said in his inimitable way.

My father was never the hands-on parent that TV sitcoms portray. With running a chain of discount stores across the country, and travels to China, India, or Taiwan to purchase stock, he didn't have time to do the usual parental things. Not that I blame Dad, or anyone else for that matter. Without his hard work, I wouldn't have the fortune I have today to create my own magazine. Besides, I really couldn't complain, Dad was always a phone call away, and if I needed to see him in person, I just had to book a time through his personal assistant, Miss Turner, and I would have him all to myself for an hour.

Don't get me wrong, dear reader, although time-poor, Dad was still a loving parent. It was the little things he did for me that really showed it. For Christmas and my birthday, I received the latest and most expensive toys: the latest Gray Nicholas cricket bat signed by the Australian Cricket team; a shiny Kookaburra four-piece ball; even an Aussie Rules Sherrin match-day ball, with a little note saying: 'Son, if you want to achieve anything in life, you need to have eyes only for your goal'. Although I never really liked sport and was too sickly for the athletic endurance of Aussie Rules, I placed it on my desk in my room and stared at it for hours, imbibing its leathery aroma.

When I was stricken with leukemia in my fourteenth year, he sent me boxing gloves signed by Mike Tyson, with a note saying: 'Fight like buggery, son. Love, Dad'. I hung the gloves above my hospital bed.

At Dad's funeral, Miss Turner mentioned this in the eulogy. There wasn't a dry eye in the church after that.

I was raised by my maternal grandmother in a big two-storey

mansion in Kew. My predominant memory from my childhood is of those great big silent rooms filled with knick-knacks, China plates, porcelain vases brimming with the scent of cut roses from the garden, and a ponderous grandfather clock chiming the hour, each hour.

Nan's house rules forbade running up and down the halls, mud, balls, big dogs with swishing tails. Instead, it was a home for tiptoeing, hushed thoughts, and pulling down books from one of the many oak bookcases and reading quietly by the window, while Bob, the gardener, worked as the rain fell into the flower beds, or the sun shone brilliantly through the jacaranda tree into the sprawling backyard. I spent many long contemplative hours of my childhood in this house, silently moving from room to room, admiring the photos of my beautiful mother adorning every mantlepiece and spare wall.

No words of mine can do justice to the beauty of my mother. Even in my purple prose moments, I have trouble capturing her essence. Suffice to say, with her long blonde hair and azure eyes, one could compare her to the most gorgeous of summer days. She was also a straight-A student and an aspiring writer. On the mantelpiece in the living room is an anthology of poems she wrote before her death.

I would love to recite to you, dear reader, some of her verse, even if just a line, but I can't. For my croaky voice could never be faithful to the rhythm of her lines, or do justice to the beauty of her words, or make real her evocative imagery. And I feel by putting my voice to her poetry, I wouldn't only destroy the meaning of her verse but kill my mother once more. Instead, I can only hum them silently to myself, like a mystical hymn.

'Your mother, if she had lived long enough, would have been more famous than your father,' said Nan. 'Could have been the next Helen Garner. Could have won the Miles Franklin.'

I always love it when Nan talks about Mum. She can still spend an entire afternoon telling little stories about her. Yet when she once talked about the Miles Franklin Award and her eyes fixed on me, the weight of the world descended upon my shoulders; and not even the stroke of Nan's fingers through my hair and her gentle 'There, there, you're not to blame. You're not to blame. It's God's fault. He needed another angel for his choir' could stop the tears flowing, or the weeping of my heart.

I apologise for writing so much about myself. You've started reading this novel in good faith. No doubt wanting to revel in one of Sam's thrilling exploits. Know how he single-handedly created a riot in the centre of Melbourne, or how he became wanted by three spy agencies, on three continents. How he was hounded by the press and attacked by a jealous husband in the middle of the street, and here I am, boring Charles Western, discussing my pointless life in detail. It's not that I consider my life more interesting than Sam's. Or that I am funnier, smarter, or more intelligent than he. I am none of those things.

Instead, I'm merely showing you the steps leading up to my meeting with Sam: setting the scene — like any novelist would do — of how an insignificant life such as mine was swept up and changed by this lovable, but terrible monster.

CHAPTER 2

Imagine

On my return to Australia, I rented a poky and musty smelling office on the seventh floor of a small, slender Spanish-styled building in Flinders Lane. Although I examined cheaper and larger premises, I took this office for sentimental reasons. The cool, dark lobby of this building, with its smell of concrete and hospital-strength disinfectant, reminded me of my visits as a little boy to my great aunt Bella, tucked away in a nursing home in Toorak.

Once the belle of Melbourne society, Aunt Bella lived the last five years of her life in a shadowy existence between this world and the next. Her greatest claim to fame, the one story she told each time I visited, was how she once dined with Salvador Dalí in Port Lligat, in Spain, and nearly consented to model for him. Whatever the truth of the matter, I've always equated this favourite aunt with Spain, and without much thought, I decided to rent an office — sandwiched between a tax accountant and a Russian travel agency — in memory to Aunt Bella, now long since gone. Even the clattering of the building's elevator reminded me of the tin of sweets she used to rattle under my nose.

I also secretly hoped that the building's soaring cracked pillars and Spanish-styled terracotta faēade, and the rusted and unused flagpole would influence the magazine's writing with a surrealist Jorge Luis Borges feel: one of my literary heroes. I half expected Salvador Dalí to jump out into the corridor on my first day, with a severed and bloody horse's head and cry: 'This is what your magazine should be about. Shock!'

In the first week, I placed a reoccurring weekly ad in the review section of *The Australian* newspaper, as well as an ad in *The Age* and the *Herald Sun*.

Fiction Writers Wanted

$100 per story

Imagine Magazine

Flat 76, Minorca Building 258/260

Flinders Lane, Melbourne 3000

Only hard-copy submissions accepted.

I didn't know how many stories I would accept, or the type of writing I would select, or even their length. In this regard, I wanted the unseen creative forces of the universe to guide me, and I'd become like a leaf carried by a current of water — my fate in the hands of the creative stream, trusting it would lead me in the right direction. Besides, I didn't have a computer, a website, a dedicated email, or even a phone connected, and these mundane issues dominated my early endeavours in those first heady days.

On the Tuesday after the first ad appeared, I received an urgent call from the post office. In the afternoon, three postal vans delivered my mail. They threw the sacks on the office floor, and as I opened each, manuscripts and A4 envelopes spilled onto my feet. Between setting up my computer, connecting the power and organising my email, I began the task of reading my way through these piles.

But as soon as I finished one story, another van arrived to deposit more bags of fiction.

By Thursday evening, I had to walk over mounds of unopened sacks of writing to get to my desk.

By Friday, my desk disappeared beneath the rising tide of unread fiction.

With my office overrun, I retired to the Young and Jackson Hotel, and beneath the nude portrait of 'Chloe', I set about reading as many submissions as possible.

The stories themselves varied considerably in subject length and quality. People — in imagination, at least — fought, argued, made love, and committed adultery. Women were raped, civilisations torn asunder, and children were ripped from their mother's breast: and that was from just one story titled: *The Massacre of Tomorrow*.

There were the obligatory hard-boiled detective stories, with world-weary, whiskey-pickled private eyes, who solved the most complex and obtuse cases involving repellent and unsavoury characters, with the barest of clues, all the while balancing angry ex-wives, or in the case of the lesbian private detective, a bitter and twisted fat circus lady ex-lover.

In the fantasy realm, writers put children on the backs of giant magical creatures and sent them flying across the night sky to distant fantastical realms, with a complex magical system, which took way too many pages to describe, and possibly a degree in ancient mythology to understand.

When the action came, our hero — aided by a wise, old mentor, a sidekick, or with one story, a talking dragon — fought hordes of dark entities with poor intent in mind, and even poorer aim. Our protagonist battled against the odds, using magical swords and other paranormal-enhanced utensils to rid the world of the evil master in control of the realm. However, the stories always ended without a final resolution, and instead, an End Note promising this was the first of a ten-part series.

In a few stories, I was transported to idyllic coastal towns with golden-sand beaches, aqua-blue waters, and a murder rate higher than Mexico City.

This was nothing compared to the killing fields of the outback, awash with the blood of Indigenous people murdered by the blood-thirsty invading Europeans. The outback was a haunting, desolate, empty landscape with a brooding question: could Australians ever be redeemed after our treatment of the First Nations people? English settlers — it seemed from the Australian writer's imagination, at least — were worse than thirteenth-century Mongol hordes that swept across Europe.

One found little imaginative relief in the inner suburbs of Australia. Here, our protagonist moved in an environment that was overrun with underworld figures, poverty, drugs, prostitution, and a hopelessness pervading every page. If the inner suburbs were bad, the suburbs were diabolical.

One dead baby narrator warned me not to be fooled by the neat and trimmed double-storey houses with well-tended gardens. Those brick fences and garden gnomes standing to attention at the front gate hid dark, dark tales of family disfunction: adultery, incest, anorexia, abortion, wife bashing, and worst of all, a proclivity to vote for the Coalition.

Here, our protagonists lived lives of quiet middle-class desperation in a cultural and spiritual wasteland. If fiction is a window to the soul, then suburban Australians are a racist, psychopathic lot, with a taste for serial killing and burying bodies in agapanthus-infested backyards.

I read some wonderful multicultural stories. Migrants from the Middle East fled indifference, poverty, discrimination, and unlawful detention. Once safely out of Australia, they found momentary contentment in their homeland, with their extended family. Their grandmothers made exotic, mouth-watering meals, and their eccentric cousins, uncles and aunts told exotic, mystical odd-ball stories that made no sense. Here our protagonist was torn between two identities. Their homeland may have been a little poor, the government a tad heavy-handed, but it had soul and history, unlike crass and commercial Australia.

Aboriginal and Torres Strait Islander peoples were wise and spiritual, while white male colonist remained cruel and intolerant. Teenage writers' heroes and heroines suffered angst and existential crisis. Female romantic writers' heroines, virginal and innocent, fell in and out of love with tall, handsome, and usually rich, pig-headed men, who were at once brooding and blunt, worldly and wise, dangerous and dirty, but on closer acquaintances were really sensitive souls able to express their love in subtle ways. By the end of the story, our heroine, with a heart beating furiously, had tamed her wild stallion of a lover to live happily and monogamously ever after.

Queer writers demanded validation from society. Feminists complained about the patriarchy. Men complained about feminists, while gay writers bitched about everything and everyone. Literary writers penned exquisitely wrought stories that were incomprehensible on the first read and even more incomprehensible after the second. Only after four pots with a naked 'Chloe' staring down, could one understand the beauty of the words, the sinuous charm of the sentences, the suggestive imagery of their prose, the exquisite body, the firm breasts, the milky naked skin … Hold on, I was looking at Chloe!

By the start of the second week, I had finally connected the phones, set up the computer and organised an email account. In the first hour, I received ten calls from writers wanting to know if I had received their pride and joy, and when they would be published and paid. I explained how I had more stories than I could possibly read. So, I assured them that as soon as I got to their story, I would call them promptly. Thus assuaged, some launched into the story behind the story. How they spent countless hours working on their masterpiece, and everyone in their family who had read it, said it would be 'the next big thing'. Many said they were working on the next great Australian novel, and would I publish excerpts? I took their details and told them I would send them a cheque for one hundred dollars, but I needed to end the call straightaway.

By the beginning of the third week, the knocking on the door began. I would have opened it, but with answering the phone, writing out the cheques, and the mail bags propped against the door, I was trapped in the office. Instead, I was reduced to screaming out, 'Come back later!'

I was saved from being permanently trapped in my office by the burly body of Boris, who with a few mighty heaves of his shoulder forced his way inside.

Boris was a large Serbian immigrant with wide, dark eyes, a hearty handshake, and a stained and smelly beaver cap. He was also the author of the story of his homeland, Kosovo, *The Massacre of Tomorrow*.

I shouted him lunch, and over pork chops with creamy mashed potato for him, a nice Waldorf salad for me, and several jugs of beer for both of us, he told me his life story.

'I come from Mitrovica, the most beautiful place in the world. Growing up, I used to go on skiing holidays with my family in the Sar Mountains. Do you ski, Charles?'

I shook my head. I hardly heard his question. I was still trying to understand what type of person would wear a beaver cap in the middle of an Australian summer. He looked as if he was ready to go hunting in the backwaters of America, not sit down to lunch in Melbourne.

'In summer,' continued Boris after taking a swig of beer, 'we used to camp along the Gazivoda Lake. Everything was perfect until Kosovo gained independence. It destroyed Serbia.' Boris banged the table so hard, other patrons stopped eating and looked towards our table.

I shook my head at the waiter when he came to refill the jug.

'I was studying Computer Science at the University of Mitrovica when the civil war broke out. There was no future in my homeland. I had an uncle living in Melbourne, so I joined him and applied for permanent residency. I even married and started a family. Are you married, Charles?'

I shook my head. The zippers of Boris' bomber jacket were momentarily dazzling my eyes in the dim light of the bar.

'Good!' said Boris, banging the table again, the cutlery once again rattling. 'Don't get married. Women only want one thing.' Boris chugged his beer.

I scratched my head. 'What's that?' I asked.

'Money,' said Boris, slapping down his glass. 'That's all men are to women. A walking bank account.' He drained the rest of his beer in one gulp before refilling his glass and taking another long scull. 'Women and divorce lawyers, I don't know which is worse,' said Boris. 'My ex-wife and her lawyer stripped me of every dollar I owned. That's why I started: "Dads Against Divorce Lawyers and Women", or DADLAW, for short. We have over 300 members and go camping one weekend every month. You should come to one of our meetings. We try to get back in touch with nature and what it means to be a man. You would like it, Charles. We have this ceremony where we pass around a talking stick, and each man tells the group how his life has been screwed by women. Our next meeting is this weekend in the Macedon Ranges. You should come, Charles.'

'I'm busy this weekend,' I said, lying, not liking camping or the thought of being surrounded by lots of angry men.

Boris sculled his new glass, then refilling it, continued his life story. 'I found out early on I didn't like my job in IT. I was earning six figures but knew it wasn't for me. What I wanted to do was write. The need is intense. I can feel it in here.' Boris placed a fist over his heart and beat his chest. 'I was living a lie in my corporate job. As if every minute not at my desk writing was a waste. That's what ended my marriage. The ex couldn't understand my need to write. She just wanted the money I made. That's all I was to her, a walking ATM machine. After my divorce last year, I resigned from my job to escape paying child support and took up writing full-time. I've written four books: *The Massacre of*

Tomorrow; Dorian's Fist; The Assassin's Revenge, and the manuscript I'm working on now, my masterpiece: *Terror at the Airport*. What I want to do, young Charles, is write airport thrillers. I see myself as the next Matthew Reilly with a large slab of James Patterson thrown in. None of this literary nonsense for me. I want to write stories that have action, have movement, colour.'

'Have you got any of your works published?'

'None,' slurred Boris as he leant across the table and looked at me squarely in the eye. 'And you and I know why.'

I moved forward too and stared into those immense, unblinking black eyes, waiting to find out what I was supposed to know, and why I was supposed to know it.

Boris, frowning at my inability to read his mind, it seemed, threw his big frame against the back of his chair and shouted, 'They hate us.'

'They do?' I asked, scratching my head.

Boris sighed, no doubt at the uncertain look clearly printed like a billboard across my face. He pounded his fist into the table. 'The people who control literature; the people who decide who is published and who is not.'

'Oh,' I said. 'And who are they?'

'I went to one of those creative writing courses at the WEA across the street,' continued Boris, 'and this female teacher kept telling me my writing needed work. It was too long and violent, and the rape scene in *The Massacre of Tomorrow* was too graphic and didn't add to the narrative of the story.' Boris pounded his fist onto the table again.

The cutlery started shaking once more.

From the corner of my eye, I noticed the female patrons shaking their heads.

Boris' voice over the course of the lunch had grown louder, more slurred with each pot of beer he drank. 'That medieval rape scene is vital. Without it, how are we to know how the two races came to hate each other. No. The real reason she hates my writing is because she hates men, all these feminists do. They want to silence us, as do the Jews who control all the publishing houses.'

I hunted for the waiter among the staring eyes. I wanted to pay the bill and get out of there. Boris' misogyny and now antisemitism had grown louder and more blatant the drunker he became. His views grated on my own sensibilities, passed down via Nan from our Church of England upbringing, to judge people not as groups but as individuals. I blushed.

Boris' garble was the only sound in the room now. Everyone had stopped the pretence of eating and now listened to Boris' tirade.

'They run all the big publishing houses. They won't publish any of my works. If it wasn't for the—'

'Boris!' I now banged the table — and with the intended outcome, Boris stopped speaking and looked at me with wide, unblinking eyes. I wasn't sure what to say next, just that I needed to get him off his current subject. 'How about coming to work for me, as a special contributor?' I whispered.

The lunch cost me $160.

The look on Boris' face? Priceless.

I didn't really want Boris working for me. I just wanted him off the subject of women and the Jewish conspiracy, and those words tumbled unexpectedly from my lips. I winced after saying them and wondered if I could take them back.

'Oh well,' I said many weeks later to Sam. 'So what if Boris was an antisemitic, misogynist. Wasn't literature littered with men who thought like Boris? Consider Dostoevsky and his antisemitism. Or Ezra Pound and his love for Italian fascism. And didn't Hemmingway lie about everything and everyone. Or consider the odious Brecht? And didn't half the writers in the 1930s barrack for the Soviet Union, the most bloody and repressive regime to ever exist. Aren't writers at once penning exquisitely wrought gems that deepen our understanding of the human condition, while at the same time supinely kissing the jackboot of some brown-shirted Nazi or communist thug? *Agreeable people, with nice thoughts*, Sam insisted much later, *are not the wellspring for great literature.* Maybe Boris was the next Aleksandr Solzhenitsyn of the airport thriller variety, and with careful mentoring, I could knock the rough edges off him. Besides, isn't diversity our greatest strength?

As Boris and I toasted the success of *Imagine*, then Chloe, with the house champagne, I thought of *Imagine* as a beacon of free speech in a land of conformity.

'I've already got some great ideas for the magazine,' said Boris. 'A change of name, for starters. We need something that screams out attention.'

As Boris expounded his ideas, I leant back and thought about the Australian literary landscape and what *Imagine* could do. There were thousands of people like Boris, who for the wrong thoughts and disagreeable words were excluded from the national narrative. *Imagine* could become a voice for the marginalised: a beacon of hope in a sea of conformity. These sentiments weren't mine (I was admiring Chloe over Boris' shoulder), however. They were the words of the pink-haired young woman with sharp brown eyes, set behind Pierre Cardin-logoed glasses, who just then appeared beside us at the table.

'Yamparti!' I hope I spelt her name correctly. That is Y.A.M., pronounced as 'Yam' followed by P.A.R.T.I., pronounced as 'party'. 'Is it Spanish?' I now slurred.

'No, I'm part Boonwurrung,' she said, showing me her Indigenous-flagged wristband and taking a seat at the table.

'You mean you have Aboriginal blood?'

'Yes.'

'You're whiter than me,' scoffed Boris.

'My grandmother was a Boonwurrung woman,' Yamparti snapped

at Boris. 'Besides, skin colour is irrelevant to the matter of race. What's important is that I identify with my people and understand and sympathise with their struggles.'

Boris snorted.

Yamparti shot Boris a quivering glare before turning her attention to me. 'You have a unique chance to make your magazine an independent voice in the culture.' Yamparti was in her sixth year of a three-year undergraduate arts degree majoring in Women Studies at Latrobe University. 'I spend most of my time writing and researching for my upcoming book,' she said as a way of explanation.

'What's it about?' I asked.

'The title is: *Australian Women Writers: Stolen Land, Stolen Bodies and the Other.*' Yamparti had obviously thought long and hard about the title, for she enunciated each word slowly and embellished them with a wave of her outstretched hand, as if reading them from a faraway billboard.

'The "Other" what?' Boris asked.

Yamparti gave Boris another fearful glare before smiling sweetly at me. 'The "Other" refers to the marginalised, the oppressed, the ones who are different in our world of uniformity. That is who we will target in *Imagine.* I mean, who you *should* target.'

As I listened to Yamparti describe her book, sprinkled with words such as, 'intersectionality', 'discourse', 'lived experience', 'privileged', 'imperialistic', 'marginalised', 'transgressing the boundaries', 'interrogating the text', I kept hearing my father's sage advice: 'Son, when you go into business, hire people smarter than you'. I was only four when he said these words, and I never understood what he meant, until this moment. He was talking about Yamparti, with an 'i' and not a 'y' at the end.

'Would you like to be the editor-in-chief, Yam,' I mumbled with intoxication.

'I never let anyone call me Yam, but in this instance, I will let you.'

She smiled as we shook hands.

Boris meanwhile settled back into his chair and shook his head imperceptibly.

That night, as I lay on my bed, with the alcohol beginning to wear off, I winced at my stupidity. What was I thinking in employing Yamparti and Boris? Two people far removed from my own world view. Inadvertently, I had broken another of my father's cardinal rules: 'Son, never make a rash decision when drunk'. Although, he said this with a more earthy prose, as he lay stretched out on the couch with a white towel over his head.

Maybe this was a blessing in disguise, I countered. Maybe it wasn't such a bad thing to employ people with a different world view from my own. Didn't my father tell me never to hire 'yes men'. Well, here was my chance. Besides, Boris had IT skills that would be invaluable in creating *Imagine's* presence on the web. As for Yamparti, she really knew how to write well, even if she tended towards academic obscurity. I had spent the last hour reading some of her fiction and non-fiction, which she had sent in as part of my initial ad. She would be perfect in shaping and editing the stories.

Yet no matter how I rationalised it, I couldn't shake the feeling I had made a mistake.

'You're weak and ineffectual, Charles Western,' Sam said to me many weeks later when all my troubles began. *'You don't like conflict and therefore let stupid but stronger characters walk all over you. You should have told them both to go take a hike.'*

'No, Sam,' I countered at the time. 'I really thought they were very nice people, and it was my job to bring out the best in them. I thought I could temper their rough edges, become their mentor. Their friends. Besides, isn't diversity an organisation's greatest strength?'

Sam had rolled his eyes and shook his head. *'Charles Western, you're a fool. A fool.'*

CHAPTER 3

THE LIBRARIAN

The next day, I shouted my new team lunch at the Young and Jackson. Here, I laid out each person's roles and duties, as well as the direction of the magazine.

'Boris, I want you to concentrate on getting the IT all sorted, including building the website and putting us onto all the social media platforms,' I said, pushing away my plate of Northern Territory barramundi. I wondered whether I should have chosen the American rib eye, like Boris. Its smell had wafted all through the restaurant, smothering all other scents, including his beaver hat, as the waiter brought it sizzling to Boris.

'What about hardware such as laptops?'

'Find out what you need, and then organise a quote. Yamparti,' I said, turning to my new pink-haired editor. 'I'd like you to work on the format of the magazine.'

Yamparti pushed aside her warm beetroot salad and took up her pen and notebook.

I closed my eyes, then recalling my overseas musing on how the magazine should look and feel, I continued, 'I want the magazine to be book-size, around fifty pages, made up of ten works of fiction. I want the magazine also distributed physically to our readers.' There was something tangible and romantic about the printed page. The smell. Yes, the smell, that's what I wanted.

'How will we solicit writing?' asked Yamparti.

'We have sacks of writing in the office. We can use this as our source.'

'I would question the quality, Charles. Also, the sheer number of stories would make it difficult to go through.'

'Let me worry about that.'

'Do we accept advertising?' she asked.

'Yes, of course,' I said without hesitation.

'I believe we should include editorial comment and criticism with the fiction,' she suggested.

'But only criticism on fiction,' I added. 'I don't want it to be political.'

'But if an essay happens to be political, but also addresses the culture, will we accept that?'

'I want the magazine to be non-political.'

Yamparti gave a faint smile before returning to her furious note-taking. 'Who will be our target audience?' she asked.

I leant back and considered the ceiling of the Young and Jackson.

'If I may suggest,' said Yamparti, leaning across the table. 'The vast majority of readers of fiction are women. My ... I mean *our* magazine has a unique opportunity to reach this untapped market of university-educated and highly intelligent women. Through careful messaging, we also have a unique opportunity to change society. Remember, in a few years these people will be society's leaders.'

'We should target everyone,' said Boris, his front chair legs snapping back to earth. 'We can't turn this magazine into a hobby horse for you and your hairy-legged friends.'

'You be careful what you say,' said Yamparti. 'There are laws against that type of language.'

'That would be right,' said Boris. 'Use the laws to silence men. Let me tell you a thing or two, *Yammy*.'

'My name is Yamparti, not Yammy.'

'Well, my lady, *Yamparti,*' sneered Boris. 'I've just spent a year in and out of divorce courts. I know every trick people like you play, and I'm not going anywhere. Isn't that right, boss?'

I nodded my head, even though I hadn't heard a word Boris or Yamparti had said since they had started bickering. I had been gazing up at the clock.

'The magazine should target everyone,' repeated Boris, jabbing at my shins with his shoes.

I jumped imperceptibly in my seat. 'Yes. That's right,' I said as the long hand of the clock finally reached ten minutes before the hour. 'It should target everyone.' I took out two 100-dollar notes and slapped them on the table. 'Now, if you'll excuse me, that's enough questions for the day, I have an important meeting I need to attend. I'll see you back at the office in a few hours.'

I left my two new employees to haggle on the finer details. As my father once told me: 'Son, the job of the boss is to set the big picture, then get the hell out of the way. Don't micromanage. That's the first lesson of business'.

'But, Dad,' I had told him at the time, 'we're building a cubby house, and they are my school friends.'

'Doesn't matter, son. Take charge by delegating.'

I pushed the cubby house, *Imagine,* and my new friends from my mind. I had a far more important task to attend to.

I took a deep breath. Today I would do it, I repeated to myself as I weaved my way through the pedestrians down Swanston Street. No more procrastination. I would be like my father and take charge. No more cowardice. I took another deep breath to compose my heart, which was rat-tat-tatting like a pedestrian crossing turned green. But instead of courage, the smell of cigars, cooked beef and chicken from shops I passed filled my lungs. The nervous rumble and tingle of the passing trams personified my own nerves. The beggars I passed on their mats reflected my state of being.

The afternoon shift had only just started as I entered the Victorian State Library.

My heart then leapt as my young librarian, with her long brunette hair and almond eyes, took her seat behind the enquiries counter.

I had visited the State Library every day since my return to Australia. I hoped the soaring architecture of the La Trobe Reading Room would inspire my creative efforts. However, the first week into this routine, I noticed this librarian at the enquiry desk on the ground floor. I was so smitten, I abandoned the reading room for the tables close to her workstation. After a week, I had even discarded my creative endeavours to stare exclusively at her over my laptop.

I had quickly learnt her routine. She worked the afternoon shift, starting around 1pm. I came each day at this time, frozen by indecision as to how to declare my love for her.

Today, I went to the closest reference shelf and took the first available book: *National Geographic Atlas of the World*. I went to pick it up; however, with my eyes fixed on her through the gaps in the shelves, and the weight of the book catching me by surprise, I let the tome slip from my grasp. The edge of the book fell onto the toes of my right foot. In the mausoleum silence of the library, I gave a piercing shriek, and hopping back on one foot, I careered into a brochure stand, sending pamphlets and perspex crashing to the floor.

After helping an unsmiling middle-aged librarian pick up the stand and brochures from the floor, I crawled across the carpet, commando-style, back into the reference aisle, pushing my atlas before me, like an SAS soldier, hoping to remain invisible to my sweet librarian.

I hid in the reference aisle for half an hour, gazing at one heavy volume after another, waiting for any memory of my transgression to subside. When I finally emerged, I limped to a seat with a clear view of the enquiry desk.

Over the next two hours, I gazed adoringly at my librarian as she attended to customer enquiries. Whenever she looked my way, I dropped my gawking to the slim and sinuous form of South America, the green lushness of the Amazon, the delicate tail of Argentina.

Finally, around four in the afternoon, the traffic to the enquiry desk slowed, then died. I took one deep breath after another, composing myself for my mission.

'Now or never,' I muttered, patting down my hair. I then rose, and taking one last deep breath, I strode over, trying to hide my limp with the manliest gait I could muster.

'Hi,' I said in a deep voice.

'Hello,' she replied.

My heart skipped several beats at the subtle French inflexion of her voice.

I stared spellbound by her almond eyes, which were glittering under the library lights. She smiled, and I realised I needed to say something. 'Charles Western.'

Silence followed.

'Is that the name of the author?' she asked in her beautiful, sing-song French accent.

I stared, opened mouthed like a goldfish out of water, now more infatuated, more terrified of her than before. 'Sorry. No. I mean … yes. I'm Charles Western and I'm also an author. Not published as yet, but hopefully soon. Not that I came to ask you that. I have a magazine.' I felt heat reach my ears.

She grinned and tilted her head, a look of incomprehension clouding her face.

'You want help finding a magazine?'

I sensed a line of people beginning to form behind me, some tapping their feet. 'No. No. I own a magazine, and I write, and my name is

Charles Western. Not that the magazine has started. Sorry, your name is?'

'Celeste,' she said, still smiling, before glancing briefly at the line now forming behind me. 'Did you have a question, Charles?'

'A question. Sorry, I don't follow. Oh yes, of course … a question.' I mentally cursed my stupidity. Why hadn't I prepared a question? I racked my brain, but all I could think of was South America and atlases. 'Do you have an atlas of South America. The Amazon looks so beautiful. Argentina, so slender.' I blushed again and wanted the earth to open beneath my feet and swallow me whole and deliver me all the way to this continent.

Celeste beamed. 'You will find it in the aisle where you knocked over the brochure stand. I hope your foot is okay?'

'It is. I'm actually dancing fit, if that's what you mean or want to do? Not that I'm asking. I came to find out about South America and the Amazon. Thank you.' And as fast as my legs could take me, I limped from the library.

Halfway down Swanston Street, I stopped on the footpath. Throwing my hands over my head, I fell to my knees and gave out a noiseless scream. I then tapped my forehead repeatedly on the cold concrete as pedestrians stepped around me.

CHAPTER 4

KAREN TIVEN

I returned in a miserable mood to a locked office and the key under the mat, with a short note explaining that both Boris and Yamparti had left for the day. Against my will, I smiled, wondering whether Yamparti and Boris had perhaps gone for a drink together. Although they bickered, they secretly loved each other. Or that was what my imagination hoped and locked on to, as way of forgetting my humiliation from the library. I could always throw them together in my daydream and spin out an amusing but unlikely story. I was so caught up in this intriguing thought, I didn't notice the woman in the corridor, until she came close, cleared her throat and asked, 'Do you work at *Imagine*?'

'I'm the owner,' I said.

'Oh, you're Charles. I'm Karen. Karen Tiven.'

My first instinct on meeting Karen Tiven was to offer her my handkerchief. Instead, I gave her my hand. She was in her late forties, rather attractive in a faded sort of way, with fair, curly hair, pale-blue eyes, and a mournful expression that suggested she had contemplated many things and found them all sad.

'I spoke to you on the phone last week,' she continued. 'You're publishing one of my stories, *Neurosis*.'

'Ah,' I said, remembering the call and placing the voice. 'Karen Tiven. You're the woman with the husband with cancer, the son uncertain of his sexuality, and the daughter who hasn't spoken to you in a year. How could I forget the call! I hope the home front has improved since then?'

'It's still the same.' Karen sighed. 'But your cheque brightened my world.'

'Thanks.' I flushed.

'I have another story you might like.'

It occurred to me I hadn't read her first story.

'You're so brave setting up a magazine for up-and-coming writers,' she said.

I took a shine to Karen upon this compliment. My dreams for unbridled success, which on my walk back from the State Library had ebbed to a solitary ember, due to my cowardice with the librarian, now flickered with new intensity. Maybe I could discover the next big talent. Maybe Karen Tiven, was it! 'I'm going for dinner at the Young and Jackson, would you care to join me?'

'Well, I really can't … you see——'

'My shout.'

'Love to.'

It was nice to share my dinner with someone at the Young and Jackson. Usually, I dined alone, before perambulating to an empty flat, stopping along the way to drink a few pots and sink into a pleasant daydream.

It was nicer still, the way Karen Tiven talked on and on about herself and her writing. I liked socialising with people who needed only an audience for a conversation and not a partner. It allowed me the luxury of sinking back in my chair and being perfectly alone in my own happy thoughts. A conversation that only required me to resubmerge once and awhile, breathe in a few words to understand the gist of their conversation, nod a few times, before diving back down to the delights of my private thoughts once more.

'It was not so much the money I appreciated,' said Karen, pushing forward her finished plate of chicken salad. 'Although, with Barry unable to work because of the chemo, I don't know how I can feed my family. It was more the validation. All those years slaving away writing … Well, I only took up writing a few years ago, but I've been thinking about it for many, many years. You see, I've always wanted to write, but growing up I never got the chance or encouragement. My parents had traditional ideas of how their children should turn out. The boys should get jobs like Dad, working with their hands, and the daughters should marry and have children. Even though I knew deep down I wanted more from life, I followed my parents' wishes and married the first good man I met and spent the next twenty years raising two children. Yet all the time, I knew I wanted more from life. I always wanted to write. Even as a child, I wrote stories and tried to get them published in the school's newsletter or the local paper, but no one ever encouraged me, and I lost confidence and stopped writing. Occasionally, I scribbled a few thoughts into a notebook. Sometimes, when miserable, I filled an entire notebook in a day. When Barry first fell ill with prostate cancer, I thought my world was ending. It was then I took up writing seriously. I joined a writing group and began to organise my notebooks. I found I had enough material in these and my diaries for four manuscripts and over ten short stories. It was after attending a writer's weekend retreat in the Dandenongs that I realised I was a writer first, and a mother and wife second. I know that sounds terrible. I'm a horrible mother for saying it, and I've spent a lot of time hating myself for even thinking it. The visiting American writer Kurt Loveheart made me realise I was more than a mother and wife. You have heard of him, no doubt?'

I shook my head.

'He's won many literary prizes for his gothic romance novels. You've heard of *Tremor; Bite;* and, *Love Among the Banshee.*' Karen paused and clearly waited for some sign of recognition.

Instead, I shook my head again.

Karen, who seemed disappointed, took a sip of her wine before continuing.

'He said the most important thing a writer can do is to keep writing. To keep at it, no matter what others thought or said. I showed him some of my stories in the lunch break. He even invited me back to his room to discuss them. He recognised my talent straightaway. He said I had story-making potential. Kurt Loveheart said that about *me!*'

I tried to look suitably impressed as Karen spoke on.

'He even hinted he could put me in front of a few agents he knew. If I didn't have duties and responsibilities, I would have returned with him to the States. Instead, I went back to Barry and laid down the law. I'm a writer, I told him as soon as he walked in the door, and I wouldn't let him or anyone else stop me from following my true calling.'

'What did Barry say?' I asked.

'He didn't say much. He looked upset by it all. He said it was the chemo, but I knew it wasn't just that. For twenty years I had played the role of dutiful wife, but now I had declared my independence, and he feared that. All men fear independent women.' Karen reclined in her seat and took another sip of her wine, then she studied me closely over the rim of her glass, the silence uncomfortable.

Was I supposed to speak? I was enjoying being alone with my thoughts but decided to ask a question. 'Have you been published?'

Karen shook her head. 'But my spiritual counsellor said I would get a book deal this year.'

'You have a spiritual counsellor? I asked, my mouth dropping slightly, glad Nan was not at the table.

'Yes, Laura Horos. She is a rapid transformational therapist, as well as one of the top spiritual manifestation practitioners in Australia. She hinted I would be published this year, but I needed to manifest on the goal while holding this special crystal.' She took from her purse a pink rose quartz. 'It's a special crystal and only cost me 300 dollars, Charles. Only 300 dollars!'

'Um. Don't you think the price is a little excessive for a quartz crystal like this?' I suggested, remembering buying the exact same stone, as a boy, for Nan for her birthday and only paying five dollars.

'She has blessed it, Charles. That is where the money is.'

'Um, don't you think … I mean … don't you think this is a scam?'

Karen frowned. 'A scam, oh no, Charles, Laura is no charlatan. In fact, she has predicted many things that have come true. She even said I would meet you.'

'Oh?'

'She said I would meet a young man in publishing. You should meet her. She is always looking for new clients. For each new introduction, I get a ten per cent discount off my next consultation. A ten per cent discount!'

'Um, no thanks,' I said. Nan always said psychics and mediums were the handmaidens of the devil, always taking money from the gullible.

We fell silent for a time. Karen taking a sip of her wine.

'What you're doing is very brave,' she then said. 'Creating a magazine and publishing new writers. This country needs more people like you.' She looked past me, with misty eyes.

'It has been a terrible twelve months.' She sniffled. 'What … with Barry's cancer diagnosis and him not being able to work. The children not talking to me. I'm struggling, Charles. Struggling.' She burst into tears.

People at the other tables stopped their eating and eyed us. I was suddenly overcome with compassion and concern for Karen.

'It has fallen on me to be the main breadwinner, but I'm struggling to find a job. No one wants to employ someone like me who has no experience in the workforce. I don't know what I'm going to do.' She buried her head in her hands and wept.

I felt so sorry for Karen. So moved by her tears that I found myself saying, 'Karen, would you like to help me put out the magazine?'

Karen's face shot out of her hands. She gazed at me open-mouthed, her tears instantly stopping.

'I need someone to read through all the stories we've received. I'll pay you a wage, of course.'

'Really?'

'Really.'

'I'd love that, Charles!' Her whole face lit up like a sparkler. 'I have so many great ideas for the magazine. Firstly, though, we need a change of name.'

CHAPTER 5

BUILDING THE MAGAZINE

Even knowing the pain and humiliation to come, the weeks leading up to the launch of the first edition of *Imagine* were some of the happiest of my life. For the first time, I had everything I ever wanted.

I owned the two-bedroom flat my mother lived in before her marriage. Although I possessed the money to purchase other grander abodes, this tiny flat in St Kilda, with its art-deco exterior, canary-yellow drapes, and faded wallpaper proved a sentimental and irresistible purchase.

Each morning after showering and eating, I liked to wander about the flat and imagine her living here, as I inhaled the musk air fresheners placed by Nan in all the rooms, (Mum's favourite scent). I visualised her sitting on the cracked leather sofa (which came with the purchase of the flat, and I dared not throw out), or imagined her lounging out on the balcony on warm days, writing her poetry as she imbibed the scent from the rows of plane trees blanketing the street in shade.

I liked to write early in the morning, guided by my mother, jotting down the random thoughts and scenes that came to mind, and I'd rearrange and rewrite the words later that night, over a few drinks, into a coherent shape.

Just before nine in the morning, three weeks before the launch, I sauntered down St Kilda Road, across the Princess Bridge into the city, admiring the pretty young girls rushing to their office jobs. At the Young and Jackson, I stopped for a cappuccino and a read of the *Herald Sun*, under the watchful eye of Chloe, before reaching the office just after ten.

Here, my friends — not colleagues or employees, but friends — were hard at work on bringing my European-created idea to life.

Boris' large, unblinking dark eyes fixated on his computer, his beaver cap hanging from the hat stand, cursing from time to time in his native tongue as he created and connected our website and social media platforms. Yamparti, with a pencil in her mouth, was compiling and editing the first edition into readable existence, while Karen picked through mounds of unread manuscripts on the floor, looking for a gem for us to publish.

I wanted to hug them all as I sat at my desk that had a big laminated sign announcing the title I had chosen for myself. 'Chief Ideas Officer'.

To show my love and appreciation for my new friends, I shouted them lunch each day in the Young and Jackson. Over our meal and drinks, I plied them with questions about their lives, wanting to quickly ingratiate myself into their worlds.

Two weeks before Easter, I unveiled the new masthead. I had tasked myself with the job of creating the visual style for the magazine. Now with us returning to the office after a heavy lunch, I decided to unveil the new look and feel for *Imagine*.

I turned on my laptop and invited my friends to watch as I pressed play on the pre-recorded speech I had spent all night preparing and recording.

Let me be truthful, dear reader, but I can't speak in public. Maybe I could speak in front of two people, but with any more than two, I shiver. My mind seizes. My heart accelerates. I'd rather rats gnaw at my face, than make a speech.

My aversion to public speaking began in the sixth grade. My class was to give a five-minute talk on the topic of our choice. I chose 'life under the sea'. I was the last to be called to speak. As each of my classmates made their speech and congregated on the other side of the stage, laughing and joking in knots, the more my palms became sweaty, the more my heart pounded until I was conscious of it in my chest. Soon, I was the only one left in the wings — a small forgotten speck of a boy, breathing in rapidly the scent of floor polish. I seemed to be there for hours.

Finally, the words 'Western, Charles' rang out over the loudspeaker. I then tiptoed on stage, tripping once on one of the theatre ropes and grazing my forehead, to the laughter of the girls in the first row. I righted myself and stared wincing out into the hushed auditorium. I could dimly make out all those expectant faces watching my every nervous twitch. The giggling girls, the bullies, the disapproving teachers. I couldn't remember my first line. Oh my god, I couldn't remember my first line. I froze. My brain wouldn't work. The smell of grilled beef and onion wafted onto the stage. Someone was eating a hamburger, and my stomach growled. I opened my mouth, but no words came out. I opened my mouth again and still nothing came out. I must have looked like a caught fish at the bottom of a boat, struggling for air, before the fillet knife put it out of its misery. I opened my mouth again. Nothing.

Panic! Alarm! A trickling sound issued at my feet. A warm, wet sensation ensued in my pants.

'Look! He's wet his pants!' One of the girls in the front row pointed.

The auditorium erupted into laughter and giggles. Their laughing, sneering faces are imprinted on my consciousness to this day. Before a teacher could put an arm around my shoulder, I fled. I ran as fast and as far as my legs and lungs would take me. I ran home to the safety of Nan's embrace.

This memory came often to me as I drifted to sleep, catapulting me to a seated position. Breathing rapidly and shallowly, I cursed my name, beat my head with a soft fist and repeated, 'I'm stupid, so bloody stupid.'

'To my friends,' the video Charles started. 'I want to thank you for accepting your position with *Imagine*. Diversity is our greatest strength.'

Yamparti imperceptibly sighed as I paused.

I noted that I slurred my words. Memo to self: don't do a video speech after half a bottle of wine.

'As you know,' video Charles continued, 'I want to publish new and interesting fiction from up-and-coming talented writers. I want to cover the literary culture of this city and country in new and fascinating ways. I wanted a masthead that reflected this vision.'

Video Charles paused again. I had really tried at this point in the recording to resist the urge to burst into tears. The wine had made me sentimental and rosy towards my three new friends. No matter what their peccadillos were, I would go on loving them, employing them no matter what they did. They were more than employees to me. They were now my buddies.

'Of course, I took your individual suggestions on board. Yamparti, with your idea of a fist wrapped with barbwire. You, Boris, with your Kalashnikov rifle and pen fashioned into a cross. And yes, you, Karen, of the lady weeping onto a page. I took them all into consideration, but in the end, I decided on the following design.' Video Charles smiled, and then slowly, the screen turned into the new masthead: the Princess Bridge with the Yarra River floating below it; the two ends of the bridge were fashioned into an inkpot with quills rising out of each end. Above this floated the word *Imagine* in gothic font.

Boris clapped. 'Marvellous, boss, the best thing I've ever seen.' His clapping was followed by Karen's, though less enthusiastically, then finally Yamparti's ... reluctantly, it seemed.

After loading the artwork onto our new website, social media pages and into the digital magazine maker, Yamparti uploaded a draft of all the stories and articles and created a table of contents. Seven short stories — two from Boris; three from Karen; plus, my intended two stories, which I would work on over the coming weeks. Yamparti provided four essays: 'The Oppression of Palestine', 'Trump's Disgrace', 'The Trans Debate', and 'Women in Fiction'.

'Are those essays related to fiction?' I asked.

'Of course,' said Yamparti. 'Of course.' She turned and fiddled with her jacket slung over her chair.

'Also, we agreed on three essays not four, and they're to be related to the writing,' I reminded her.

'They are really just small essays, Charles,' she replied.

Boris' foot hit my shin. Boris' foot was right. I needed to act.

CHAPTER 6

Human Resourcing at Imagine

'Firstly, Charles, I want to thank you for the opportunity to be the editor of your magazine. It's an honour and privilege,' said Yamparti, finishing her plate of sweet and sour cauliflower at a vegetarian cooperative restaurant close to our office.

It was the day after the launch of the masthead. For our meeting, I had offered to shout her a meal in any restaurant of her choosing. She had chosen this dimly lit place in an obscure alleyway, which was run by students, or was it an obscure religious cult — I couldn't tell, but by the look of the staff, fashion sense and good hygiene weren't high on the syllabus or their pantheon of virtues.

I had called the meeting to discuss editorial direction. Or more ostensibly, the essays written by Yamparti and inserted into the magazine. I had read them last night at the Young and Jackson while having dinner and found none of them related, in any way, to a dissertation of literature nor the culture, but they were merely political diatribes on one topic or another.

'I have … I mean *we* have a unique opportunity to influence the culture of this city,' continued Yamparti. 'You're one of a kind, Charles.

Not many people in your position would spend money setting up a new magazine, especially a literary one. The world needs more people like you.'

I blushed what I knew was the colour of the uneaten beetroots on my plate. Feeling this warm praise beginning to cloud my judgement and the message I needed to convey, I quickly recalled one of my father's sagest pieces of advice: 'Son, to succeed, you need to ignore the flatterers as well as the knockers'. He had told me this after I held up my fingerpainting following a day at kindergarten and raved how much Miss Richmond liked it. I remember how deflated I was upon receiving this piece of advice, but as I grew older, I understood the importance of being 'even tempered'.

'I really want to commit to this magazine full time,' she continued. 'But I just want to ensure we are on the same page.'

'I'm glad that you want to be on the same page, that's why I called this meeting,' I said, glad of the chance to interrupt her waffling monologue and come to the point. 'Your essays don't seem related to fiction or culture,' I advised. 'As already indicated, we're to publish new and original fiction, plus only *three* essays, which all need to relate to literature. We shouldn't be writing about US or Middle Eastern politics.'

'I know. I know,' said Yamparti. 'But fiction doesn't live in a vacuum from the wider political environment.'

'That may be true, but our focus is on fiction.'

'But there are so many marginalised voices *Imagine* can help,' cried Yamparti.

All through the meal, my gaze kept falling from her face to all the badges and pins gleaming in the dim light on Yamparti's denim jacket, like medals on a Russian Marshall at a May Day parade: Palestinian Rights; Women's Rights; Trans Rights. Treaty Now! Save the Planet! Save the Rainforest! So many 'rights' to be had, so many things to be saved. I had wondered, while chewing unhappily on my meal, where she found the time to support them all, what with studying, writing her book and editing a magazine.

Well, it was out now. She wanted to use *Imagine* as a platform for these causes.

'It shouldn't crowd out the fiction,' I said.

'We can gain instant credibility by supporting important causes.'

'I don't want us to be political at all.'

'Of course, Charles, of course. I really don't want to comment on politics at all, but the world's in such a mess that we need to be politically active.'

'Again, I don't want to crowd out the intent of the magazine, which is works from up-and-coming writers,' I said louder, a note of exasperation in my voice. I wondered whether Yamparti understood my vision at all.

'But I have five essays already loaded.'

'Five!'

'They're very small, and I'll re-edit them tomorrow to include discussion on literature.'

I crossed my arms. Did I really want this fight now? I felt drained and helpless whenever I fought with people, always taking the easiest and simplest option in any conflict — which was to concede and move on to the next point. 'Okay,' I finally said, exhaling. 'We'll run the essays. But from then on, three only,' I said, showing three fingers, to hammer home my point. 'But for the next edition, all essays must be about literature and not politics.'

'Of course, Charles. I understand,' said Yamparti, imperceptibly smiling.

We fell silent. Yamparti sipping her dairy-free dalgona coffee while I — feeling diminished and cowardly for taking the path of least resistance to land on a tawdry compromise — tried to finish one of my beetroot balls.

I realised then that my capitulation was in part due to being still hungry and wanting to end this meeting as quickly as possible. My stomach growled unsatisfied. I had ordered the colourful beet salad with carrot, quinoa and spinach, misreading the beet for beef, believing they catered also for non-vegetarians. What came from the kitchen was a few potato-sized beetroots, surrounded by crunchy green slime.

I was debating whether to buy a souvlaki or a beef kebab on my way home when Yamparti started again.

'Now that that is settled, we need to discuss Boris and Karen.'

'What about them?' I asked.

'I'd like to replace them both with someone I know from my squat in Brunswick. A far better writer, Kim Wheoki. They, is non-binary, a woman of colour and has already written ze first novel.'

'They? Excuse me, how many do you want to employ?' These words, tinged with shock and puzzlement, had tumbled unexpectantly from my mouth.

'No, Kim's pronouns are "they" and "ze", and "they" is non-binary.'

'We're talking of more than one person, right?'

'No. No,' said Yamparti, sighing and slapping the table. 'As a CIS white male, you have a lot to—' She stopped and took a deep breath before tattooing a smile on her face. 'They'll give our magazine considerable credibility.'

It took me longer to digest the last few sentences from Yamparti than the mash of burnt cauliflower in cream sauce, which came as an entrée. I had masticated this meal slowly and without much joy, much like Yamparti's words. Non-binary what? Was that a man who was a woman, or a woman that was a man? Were there multiple people in this deal? Yamparti lived in a squat? CIS male?

'Firstly, I'm not a sissy, and secondly, you want to get rid of Boris and Karen?' I cried, latching onto the only thing that made any sense out of her last few sentences.

A few of the poorly dressed and bizarre-looking people in the room stopped their chewing and stared our way.

'Firstly, Boris is a white supremacist, as well as being a poor writer,' imparted Yamparti. 'He gave me a ten-thousand-word story on a contract killer that makes no sense, as well as being filled with sexist stereotypes and a violent assault.'

'Can't you edit it?

'Edit it? It doesn't have any plot to edit, just a lot of groups randomly shooting at one another and having sex. We can't publish it. We'll be a laughing-stock.'

'Look, I know Boris annoys people, and he's a little chauvinistic—'

'A *little* chauvinistic! The man is a racist homophobe, and my … I mean *your* magazine shouldn't pander to his hate, vile misogyny, and antisemitism.'

'Aren't the Palestinians also antisemite?' I said, pointing to one of her badges.

'How can you equate a misogynist, racist like Boris, with the Palestinians under occupation in their own homeland.'

'How so …' I said, genuinely interested in understanding the comparison. I really did like debate.

But Yamparti shook her head and scowled before changing tact. 'Karen needs to go, as well.'

'First you want to get rid of Boris and now Karen. That's two thirds of the current staff. Next, you'll want to get rid of me.' I laughed nervously.

Yamparti, however, remained stony-faced. 'She's not doing her job correctly.'

'What do you mean?'

'She's not reading through any of the manuscripts. Instead, she keeps giving me her stories to put into the magazine.'

'I'll have a word with her, but I can't fire her. She has a family to support.'

'You're too nice, Charles. You're letting people like Boris and Karen take advantage of you. They don't deserve your compassion.'

'I can't do it.'

'I know it's hard for a person like you to say no,' said Yamparti, leaning forward. 'That's why I say go away for a few days and I'll do the job.'

'I know you are very passionate about this subject, Yamparti, but I can't let you sack them. I want to create a magazine with a diverse range of views and talents. As we all know, diversity is our greatest strength,' I said, repeating that well-worn and glib phrase, which I had heard countless commentators and academics on TV and in print repeat. And now I repeated it to someone I knew who would appreciate my approach to diversifying thought in the culture. Wasn't that what people like Yamparti wanted?

But Yamparti stared at me for a long time, with the same look Nan had when I told her I was thinking of dying my hair green.

'She's turning the magazine into a joke,' said Boris over coffee in one of the laneway cafés. 'It's becoming a platform for all her hairy-legged friends at university.'

Even with the sound of plates and saucers being shuffled like cards in one of the nearby eateries, the beeps of trucks reversing in Flinders Lane, and the hundred different conversations coalescing into one wall of noise, Boris' voice still stood out, punctuating the cacophony of sound, drawing attention from nearby tables.

'You need to stand up to her or she'll take over the entire magazine, pushing you out. Have you read this?' He waved in the air the short five-page essay on 'Intersectionality' Yamparti had provided to Boris, Karen and me. My copy came with an underlining on the section related to the correct use of pronouns.

I nodded.

'This is the type of leftist gobbledygook she is pushing in the office.

Also, she's putting essays into the magazine. Have you read them?'

'I've asked her to edit them,' I said.

'Really, Charles, you're letting her get away with murder,' said Boris. 'She really is—'

'I want to talk to you about a delicate matter,' I interrupted Boris, wanting to move the conversation to the intended reason for this impromptu private meeting. 'How shall I say this,' I started then stopped. I then stirred my coffee, trying to think of the best way to approach the subject.

Boris' eyes widened. I noted this about him. It seemed he liked to listen through his eyes.

'I know you meant nothing by it, and you were only trying to illustrate your scars from knee surgery, but next time, can you keep your pants on in the office.'

'What? I don't understand.'

'The other day … You took off your pants in the office to show me your knee injury from fencing.'

'That bitch Yamparti,' said Boris, his voice slicing through the racket of sound.

Several of the clientele nearby stopped their conversation and stared in our direction.

'I know you meant nothing by it, but others in the office didn't appreciate it,' I said, not adding that one of those people happened to be me. I never liked nudity, feeling self-conscious in the change rooms at school as I undressed. Not liking to look at other boys' bodies as a comparison. Yet Boris jumped to Yamparti as the reason for this conversation.

'Really, Charles. You can't let Yamparti boss you around. Be a man about this.'

'All I ask is that you keep your pants on in the office.'

Boris crossed his arms and frowned.

As for Karen, my little chat didn't go any better than with Boris.

'That bitch Yamparti! I'm sorry, Charles, I know I shouldn't speak badly of your editor-in-chief,' said Karen over her skinny latte in a Flinders Lane café the next day. 'No, damn it, I've put up with people trying to put me down for too long, and I'm not letting that woman get the better of me. Laura has counselled me to be strong and vent. Says it is the only way to free myself of her bad energy.' Karen leant back on her seat, closed her eyes and took a deep breath before exhaling loudly. Finally, she opened her eyes and expressed, 'She starts bossing me around as soon as you leave the office. "Get on the computer and make the following changes to this story," she barks. When I tell her I don't take orders from her, only from you, she screams, "You will do as you're told".' The tears Karen so valiantly seemed to fight to keep down now bubbled to the surface. 'I don't need to be spoken to like that. I've got a sick husband to look after, children to feed. Besides, I'm a writer not a reader, and I need time to write, not wade through other people's stories.' Karen started sobbing uncontrollably.

The patrons at other tables looked at Karen, then their disapproving eyes turned to me.

'And when I show her a good story for the magazine ...' Karen sniffed after composing herself. 'She dismisses them out of hand. Says they're either too long, or too boring, or don't fit in with the ideals of the magazine. *Diagnosis* is the perfect opening story for the first edition. I consider it my best work so far. I don't want to blow my own trumpet, Charles, but my creative writing teacher, Jillian Box ... You've heard of her, Charles?'

I shook my head.

'She's a very distinguished Australian writer. She's the author of *Love and Other Terminal Diseases*.' Karen stopped and clearly waited, yet again, for a flicker of recognition.

I scratched my head, as I had numerous times when she'd mentioned someone from her writing posse.

'She's won the 2004 Echuca Short Fiction Award and the 2015 Dan Murphy fellowship prize for poetry.' Karen stopped and judged my expression once more; no doubt waiting for a cry of recognition or an impressed exclamation.

I nodded and faked a flicker of excitement. Nan would be pleased with my manners.

'She said in front of the class that *Diagnosis* showed rare perception of what some women faced when their loved one died of a terminal illness. She even tied in my story with her own husband's death from bowel cancer. Jillian Box tied her own life story with mine! I call that connecting through fiction. In fact, she was so impressed with my story, she invited me to one of her master classes in Eltham. Only sixty of her best students attended, Charles. Only sixty.' Karen beamed like the sun at sunset, until a dark cloud of memory, one called 'Yamparti', no doubt, passed over her triumphant thoughts of literary success. She then frowned. 'That university know-nothing says *Diagnosis* is too long and boring. What nonsense. These days, you can't say anything important under less than ten thousand words. You must help me, Charles.'

I leant back in my chair and *mmmmed*.

'You're brilliant, Charles,'

'Okay, let's do it. We'll publish it as a serial.'

'First story in the magazine with a lead on the front cover?'

'Okay, why not.'

'Wonderful! Also ... is it possible to work only a few hours in the afternoons, Charles. I'll come in, in the morning, but I need the afternoons to write.'

'Sure, why not.' I forced the corners of my mouth up.

Although I struggled with my friends in the quotidian reality of the here and now, in my imagination, I had transformed their whispered back-biting into comedy potential. On my way to work, I daydreamed about a sitcom based on a magazine called *Imagine* …

Boris bursts through the office door. He pauses as the studio audience claps. 'Boss! Boss! I've found the next big thing.' (Boris is very excitable.)

'You met another girl in a bar,' says Yamparti, folding her arms.

(Canned laughter)

Boris is a big bear of a man, crazy, impulsive, always bursting in and out of doors.

Then there is Yamparti: learned, controlling, pretentious and conservative. Yet, her tough manner is only a facade. Beneath her biting tongue, there is a ten-year-old girl still crying the night her daddy left her mummy for another woman. All her need to control comes from a desire to unscramble the broken home of her childhood. All her hatred of men, and Boris in particular, is her inability to trust her father again.

Boris and Yamparti secretly love one another.

Yes, that was it. All good TV shows needed a love interest, one that was never consummated, of course.

There is also the eccentric, neurotic and gullible Karen Tiven. Always with some family drama to attend to, always falling under the spell of some crazy guru or cult. To the consternation of her colleagues and especially her boss, Charles Western, she tries to change the direction of the magazine to the bent of her newfound obsession.

Then there is Charles Western, all-round good guy, a little goofy, trying to put out a magazine, but with no help from his three crazy employees. A Jerry Seinfeld -like character: the sane nucleus around which the other eccentric characters throw out their lines.

In this daydream, I imagined their futures after the success of the sitcom, and how I would be credited …

Karen on *Oprah*, discussing her books, her bedridden husband, her troubled son, and her wayward daughter. A scan of the studio audience as Karen rakes over the intricate details of her personal life, revealing the people who will buy Karen's books:

nodding middle-class women, like her, with troubled families and harrowing personal stories of their own to tell and share.

On Amazon's bestseller list is Boris Petrović, the new Matthew Reilly, and his novel: *Terror at the Airport*. The front cover is of a bomb surrounded by planes.

As for Yamparti, she is already ensconced with a leading university. Whenever an important issue arises, there is Yamparti's head on the Australian Broadcasting Commission, her name in print with all the leading left-wing newspapers. 'Leading academic, Yamparti Jones, today called on the Australian Government to start doing more for artists with disabilities.'

Not that they ever mention me by name. That is too egotistical, and I am a modest person by nature. Instead, my pleasure is to see their success.

Of course, their biographers know the full story. How they first found success with *Imagine*. How the eccentric owner discovered their talents and shaped their careers; the man they saw as their mentor and dearest friend.

The golden-haired investigative journalist, who comes to write my biography understands it all. 'Charles Western, modest and shy, also a little eccentric', her book mentions. 'Wildly handsome, too, with hazel eyes and blonde hair. He also smells of earth after rain, and lemons' …

Or that was what Nan claimed I smelt like, and my biography would repeat.

In my mind's eye …

I amble down Collins Street, with her on my arm. It's a cool April night. We step out of the Princess Theatre from a late performance of the musical, *Terror at the Airport,* written by Boris Petrović, music by Björn Ulvaeus, from Abba. City lights like sparklers cut through the mist, shrouding the tall office buildings. Our footfall echoes against the faded splendour of the Melbourne Club, as tintinnabulating trams rumble past.

At the Baptist Church we stop, and I turn to her, and she is now Celeste from the library. I take her in my arms. We kiss, then she whispers to me, 'Charles. Charles. Charles …'

I snapped out of this intoxicating daydream to find that in my mind's absence, my feet had taken me to the enquiry desk of the State Library, hoping against all hope that I might have had the courage to ask Celeste out. 'Oh yes, Celeste. How are you?'

'I'm fine. Is the foot better, Charles?'

'My foot? My foot?'

'You dropped a book on it and knocked over a brochure stand last week.'

'Oh, my foot. Of course, of course,' I stammered. 'It's fighting fit. Perfect, really. Never been better. I could dance on it, if that's what you mean? If that is what you want to do? Not that I'm asking or should ask.' I stopped and blushed as a line formed at my back, increasing my nervousness; my mind was beginning to race like my heart — out of control.

Celeste's beautiful eyes darted briefly to consider the line, before she said, 'Do you have a question, Charles?'

I had many questions. Why was she so beautiful? Why couldn't I keep my eyes off her? Would she ever go out with me? Would she ever let me kiss her? Did she understand her effect on me? But instead, I hummed like a bee.

Celeste smiled.

I then took another deep breath and continued to *um,* this time like a Tibetan monk in meditation.

'Do you have a question?' she asked, glancing imperceptibly at the line behind me.

'I have a magazine.' I finally gulped.

Celeste tilted her head as if trying to read my thoughts. She also seemed to be waiting for something else. Some other piece of information.

Breaking free of the trance induced by her eyes (I had noted the colour of one iris was paler than the other), I gave her a draft copy of the first edition of *Imagine.*

She looked at the front cover. 'Are you looking for this publication?' she asked.

'No. No. It's the draft of my new magazine. I'm the owner. Also, I'm one of the contributors.' I pointed to my name on the front cover beneath a story I had written for the first addition: 'A Mother's Love'.

'You want the library to keep it?'

'No. No. Not the library, it's for you,' I said. 'I want you to have it. It's a draft of the first issue. It's a little rough. And if you want me to change anything, anything at all, let me know. When it comes out, I'll bring you the first copy.'

Her smile widened, and I weakened, becoming petrified. What if she didn't like my story? Now was the time to ask her out. Now was the time. 'Celeste, there is something else I must ask you,' I said, staring into those eyes, losing myself in their beauty, their perfection.

'Celeste, will you … will you … will you point me to books on … on … on Tibetan folk dancing.' Shoot me! Someone please shoot me, now! Folk dancing, really!

Celeste's face creased with clear incomprehension then stiffened into the formal professionalism of her trade as she directed me to the correct floor and aisle.

I left without following her directions, scurrying from the library and slumping beneath the statue of Redmond Barry. What was I thinking? Tibetan folk dancing. What was wrong with me? Why was I so pathetic?

I eventually rose to my feet, determined to rush back into the library and ask her out. But as I took my first step for this purpose, a wave of nerves washed over me and instead, I turned. Like a scared little boy, I slunk back to the office, with a bent head.

CHAPTER 7

BORIS' MONEY-MAKING IDEA

'So, Boris, you wanted to speak to me about an urgent matter,' I said, tucking into my lamb rack at the Young and Jackson. It was the Wednesday evening before Easter, and Boris had wanted to meet me one-on-one after our last meeting in the café. The one about keeping his pants on.

'I'm glad of the opportunity to meet you privately,' said Boris as the waiter placed before him his sizzling spiced kangaroo with bush tomatoes, replacing his regulation knife with a steak one. 'Firstly, I want to thank you for the opportunity to work for your magazine. If Yamparti wasn't the "editor", it would be the dream job.' He began cutting his kangaroo.

I then watched him chew, and so I continued with the point I had to make, 'As we already explained, we needed to cut your story about the contract killer to fit it into the magazine. All stories need to be no more than 2000 words in length, and you gave us one 10,000 words long.' I should have chosen the spiced kangaroo instead of the lamb rack. The scent of Boris' meals always overpowered mine when we ate together, and I again regretted my choice.

'What I wanted to say couldn't be expressed in that number of words, but that's not the reason I wanted to chat with you,' he advised me.

'Oh.'

He then put down his cutlery and appeared serious. 'I have a money-making idea. One that a smart man like you would jump at.'

'I'm all ears?' I said, taking a sip of my beer.

'Instead of sinking all your cash into this magazine, you should set up your own publishing venture.'

'What do you mean?' I asked before taking a mouthful of beans with the lamb.

'Become a literary broker.'

'I still don't know what you mean?'

'You finance up-and-coming novelists. Help them publish their works online and split the profits with them.'

'You mean help them self-publish?'

'Exactly. All you need to do is find writers that cater for the popular market. Ones that people want to read, then back them into print.'

'Do you know any up-and-coming authors I could invest in?'

Boris laughed. 'You're kidding, boss,' he said, dropping his fork, which clattered on the edge of his plate.

I knitted my eyebrows.

'I'm your man, boss,' he said, leaning forward and beating his chest.

'Oh?'

'You've finished reading the final draft I sent you of *Terror at the Airport*?'

'Well, yes.'

'Tell me that it isn't the best thriller you've read? It would be perfect for our little venture. You help me self-publish and market it, and I can promise you six-figure sales.'

'Six figures?' I exclaimed, unable to hide my incredulity.

'The book's an instant bestseller. I'm sure to be offered money for the film rights. I've put that in the contract I've drafted.'

'You've drafted a contract?' I gasped.

'Can't you see Tom Cruise playing the part of the hero, Terrence Nightingale? Tell me you can see it?'

'Um. Well. Um.'

'Russell Crowe, then?'

'Um.'

Boris stiffened in his seat.

My attention was drawn to his white knuckles as he squeezed the steak knife and pointed it in my direction.

'You did read it?'

'I did,' I said, putting down my fork and leafing absent-mindedly through the 700-page manuscript on the table, which I had lugged around with me over the last few weeks. I had been frog-marching my way through it at lunch breaks, at the pub on the way home from the office, and the early hours of the morning when I couldn't sleep. Its weight had proved also useful as a bedroom doorstop last night, letting in a pleasant cross-breeze from the living room window. 'I've nearly finished it,' I said, choosing my words carefully. 'Only fifty pages to go, I think, and um … well … you see …'

'I don't understand your hesitancy. If I was in your position, I would pour all my money into its publication.'

I scratched my head and opened the manuscript to a random page, not daring to look up into those unblinking eyes, or the serrated edge of his knife, glistening under the lights of the room. 'It's … Well …'

'It's what?' asked Boris, leaning forward, the knife still pointed in my direction.

'I'm a little confused about the plot.'

'Confused?' queried Boris, frowning. 'There's nothing confusing about it. Bad guys try to take over airport. Terrence Nightingale, ex-Australian SAS soldier, saves the day.'

'Why are the bad guys attacking Moorabbin Airport. Don't you think it's a little out of the way? A little small.'

'They want to send a message to the other world powers. Moorabbin is only the beginning.'

'I got that about the Islamic terrorists. But I don't understand why Russian special forces are also attacking the airport at the same time?'

'You didn't read the book closely, did you!' said Boris, now using his knife to jab three times in my direction. 'To kidnap the inventor of the quantum entanglement bomb, Dr Sidorov, as he took off in his Cessna to return to his lair on French Island, of course.'

'Ah, yes, the quantum laser bomb … able to destroy any city merely by destroying one stone taken from the city centre. I got that, but I thought the Chinese were after Dr Sidorov.'

'No. No,' said Boris, waving this ridiculous assertion away with a swish of his knife. 'The Chinese are attacking Australia as part of their joint invasion with the Indonesians.'

'There are Indonesians?' I cried. I spoke too loudly, for a few people in the restaurant looked up from their food and stared.

'The Indonesians are attacking the top end,' clarified Boris. 'That was at the beginning of chapter twelve.'

'That now explains why the novel jumped from Melbourne to Broome without warning. But I thought they were Chinese.'

'No. No,' said a now clearly irritated Boris. 'The Chinese have their sights set on capturing Moorabbin Airport and the military research facility within its grounds.'

I took up the manuscript again and flicked randomly through pages, looking for any mention of a top-secret military research facility.' 'Don't you think there is too much going on in your novel?" I asked. 'All these different groups shooting at each other. It's difficult to know what's happening, and who's attacking who.'

'That's the whole point, boss,' said Boris. 'When you come to the last chapter, all is revealed.'

'I hope to have that pleasure tonight,' I said without enthusiasm.

'It's only in the last few pages that we find out who has been orchestrating these various actors all along.' Boris looked at each table on either side, then leaning forward like a little boy who couldn't wait for Christmas, he whispered, 'I don't want to spoil it. But a smart guy like you has probably already guessed it by now. The whole thing was a covert CIA operation.'

I wobbled in my seat. My mouth then dropped as I slapped my forehead with my open palm.'

'Quite the twist, eh?' said Boris.

'I'll say,' I said, shaking my head.

'I bet you didn't see that coming?'

'Not at all,' I said.

'I hope I didn't spoil the surprise?'

'No. No … not at all.' I really wanted to ask: why? Why on earth where the CIA manipulating all these people? But staring into Boris' childlike eyes, I thought, no answer, no matter how plausible, could be enough. Instead, I attempted another tact. 'You're going to have to edit your manuscript.'

'Edit it?' replied an open-mouthed Boris.

'Don't you think at 700 pages that it's a tad too long, also confusing … with so many things happening?'

'I don't know what you mean, it's under two hundred thousand words. Besides, it took me a whole three months to write.'

'You have almost ninety pages dedicated to Terrence and his divorce.' I didn't add how I fell asleep twice through these passages.

'I wanted to show not only the professional obstacles he faced, but also the emotional and personal pressures he was under.'

'Don't you think calling Terrence's ex-wife lawyer a femo-Nazis a tad melodramatic, not to mention one dimensional characterisation?'

'I wanted to show how the hero has enemies on all sides.'

'You also call the Russian protagonist, Mikhail Petrov, a vodka-drinking, big bear of a man, and you describe Fang Shoo, your Chinese commander's countenance, as inscrutable. Don't you think these racial stereotypes detract from your story?'

'You have no feel for the airport thriller genre, Charles. That's what the reader wants. What they expect. Now, I have a contract here for you to sign.' He took from his bag a document and a pen and handed them over.

I flicked through the pages. 'This is an eighty-twenty split in your favour, Boris. With a fifty per cent advance.'

'I'm the one providing the product, Charles. You're just the financier.'

'If you don't mind, I'd like to think it over.'

'You need to make up your mind soon, Charles,' said Boris with his knife still pointed in my direction. 'This is a once-in-a-lifetime opportunity.'

'Let me come back to you after Easter.'

'I don't understand your hesitancy,' he said, shaking his head and taking a stab of his meal.

I fell back into my seat and sculled the rest of my beer, wondering how I could possibly avoid this contract, or whether I had the guts to even say no. I wanted to keep Boris as a friend, but I didn't want to enter into any contract either. I was such a miserable coward. I would sign. I would be too cowardly to resist.

As Sam said much later: *'Charles, you will do anything to keep a friend.'*

CHAPTER 8

EASTER

Easter came and I spent Good Friday with Nan. In the morning, we went to church, and as the day also coincided with my birthday, we visited Mum at the Boroondara Cemetery, as we did every year, to place a single white rose upon her grave.

In the afternoon, we visited one of Mum's old school friends from ballet, and together, Nan and Janet discussed the old days.

'She was a talented ballerina,' said Nan. 'Her instructor said she could have been one of the finest dancers in the state.'

After our visit, Nan prepared one of my favourite dishes: salmon with dill-mustard sauce. I uncorked a Yarra Valley pinot noir to complement it, and put on Nan's favourite composer, Chopin.

'What are you doing with yourself these days, Charles?' she asked.

'I've started a literary magazine.'

'Is there any money in that?'

'It's not about the money. It's about the writing and the friendships. I've made some nice friends since starting the magazine.' I went on to explain in detail the eccentric peccadilloes of Yamparti, Boris and Karen.

As I talked about my new friends, Nan's lined face sagged. The woman who raised me, fed me, loved me when I thought no one else would, and hugged me when I believed no one else cared, now looked sad, now looked worried. I didn't want to make Nan unhappy, for she was my world. Yet here she was with a worried look on her face.

'You will be careful, dear,' she said.

I downed my glass of pinot in one gulp as the music stopped.

'I don't want them taking advantage of my boy.'

'They're my friends, Nan. My friends.' I realised I said this more angrily than I really was.

'You are taking your medication, Charles?'

'I don't want to discuss it.'

'But Dr Regi said it was important—'

'I said I don't want to talk about it,' I replied, taking the bottle and refilling my glass, which overflowed and spilled onto the table.

Nan rose and took away the bottle. She then brought back a towel from the kitchen, which she used to wipe away the stain.

I stared at my food and sipped my wine. The relentless tick, tick of the grandfather clock was audible and thick in the subsequent silence.

'I haven't forgotten what day it is,' said Nan, finally. She rose again and took a wrapped present from the mantlepiece. 'Happy birthday, Charles.' She placed a kiss on my brow and gave me a big hug.

I squeezed her tightly in turn before opening the card to the following:

To the Greatest Grandson in all the World.

May you write many stories with it.

I then opened the present, which was no bigger than my hand. It was a Schaeffer pen. I kissed Nan. 'I'll always use it and write a hundred stories with it,' I said.

Nan started Chopin again ...

Then I caught my happiness in the window reflection. A look I knew so well appears in nan's eyes.

'I felt it too.'

We ate in silence after that, the void filled with the sound of cutlery on China, the grandfather clock ticking, the wafting and ambling ivory of Chopin's Fantaisie in F minor, and Nan's sniffles.

You didn't need to look up from your plate to know what the solitary flickering candle flame exposes upon her face: the watery eyes, the tear tracking down her cheeks, dissolving into grief. Yes, today is a special day for you, one honouring the sacrifice of a very special person. One who gave their life for yours.

Later, after Nan goes to bed, you will retrieve the bottle she took away from the table, plus another bottle. You know all her hiding spots. In the meantime, you lift your glass to your mother's portrait in salutation, and vow to get roaring drunk.

CHAPTER 9

A NEW STORY

The next morning, I woke in my old bed to a clear, fine day, a pounding headache, and a need to write. The words poured out after breakfast. Only half conscious of what I wrote and why, I let the words lead wherever they may. I wrote to Bach and the ticking of the grandfather clock marking the seconds and then the hours. Whenever I looked up, my mother implored me with a smile, 'You can do it, Charles. You can do it.'

Meanwhile, black and white photographed ancestors from their frames fixed me with disapproving stares. 'Why are you writing? Why aren't you out working? Get out in the sunshine, it will make a man of you.'

You cover their sour expressions with a tea towel and push on, letting the current of the story take you wherever it wants.

By Sunday afternoon, I discovered the plot of my story ...

A little boy waits at the airport for his mother's flight to come in. She has been away many years, and the little boy, sick with loneliness, is excited, soaking in everything he sees about him.

Holding his grandfather's hand, he presses his nose to the window, and through a fogging pane, he watches his mother's plane taxi to the arrival gate. It takes an eternity.

Finally, a door opens, and through a crush of people, he sees his mother. He launches himself into her arms, losing himself in her embrace, the smell of her perfume, the caress of her fingers.

All Easter, I wrote, adding, deleting, and refining the story, until I could do no more.

I ran to the office on Tuesday morning, my hands shaking as I showed firstly Boris, then Yamparti, and finally Karen my new story. I drank in their facial expressions as they read, imagining by the twitch of their eyes where they might be within the narrative.

'You're a genius, boss. No doubt about it,' said Boris. 'None of this arty farty nonsense. I like how the main character Trevor—'

'The boy is called Tom,' I corrected.

'Tom, that's right. How he misses his girlfriend.'

'His mother,' I corrected.

'His mother … that's right. I liked how Tom loves his mother so much he's willing to hug and kiss her as if he was still a little boy.'

'He is a little boy,' I said.

'Of course,' said Boris. 'But let me make one suggestion, you should have a situation in the airport: a terrorist attack or drug smugglers, maybe even a shootout.'

'Okay, let me think about it,' I said, grabbing back my story.

'It's wonderful. It's definitely going in this edition,' said Yamparti. 'But can I suggest making the story not about a little boy, but a Middle Eastern girl who is reunited with her mother, after being deported by a heartless conservative government. That would be even more poignant.'

'Err, maybe …' I said.

'Such a vivid imagination,' said Karen, putting down my story and taking a sip of her skinny latte, while we were in one of the outdoor cafés in Flinders Lane. The air was heavy with the chatter of sparrows and the scent of toasted bagels and coffee. 'In fact, it reminds me of a story Kade would write. He's the male protagonist in my manuscript: *Under a Samoan Sky*. You did receive the manuscript in the mail, along with all my others.'

'I did, thanks,' I replied.

'I haven't told anyone this,' said Karen, looking firstly at one table close by, then the others.

The people on these tables were too absorbed in their own conversations to be interested in the revelations of a middle-aged female writer.

'*Under a Samoan Sky* is based on a true story.' She leant across the table before continuing in a low tone, 'I won a cruise to Samoa, through a competition. Barry couldn't go because of work, so I went alone. Well, I met someone. Kane was a creative writing teacher at the University of Arkansas. He also wrote science fiction stories like this.' She picked up my story and waved it like a handkerchief. 'I showed him several of my stories, and one thing led to another.' She stopped and sighed and stared dreamily over my shoulder, as if she was reliving the cruise once more. The limitless horizon, the smell of the sea, the twinkling lights of the deck, those steamy tropical sunsets while held in the embrace of her lover. Her eyes became watery bubbles before she returned her gaze to mine. 'I felt terribly guilty, of course. He was married. I was married. He wanted me to come to the United States. He would divorce his wife, but I couldn't leave Barry. So, I returned to Australia and did the only thing I could do to lessen the pain. I threw the experience into *Under a Samoan Sky*. Laura made me realise Kane was my twin flame. My twin flame, Charles!'

I sighed, and placing my head on my hand, I retreated inside my mind and relived my story once more, adding and subtracting to it as I pleased, while Karen prattled on and on about her affair.

CHAPTER 10

Ki Goonawanda

After Easter, with Karen refusing to read through the manuscripts and stories, Yamparti initiated a ruthless regime at the office. Boris collected all the sacks of unread fiction, carried them downstairs and threw them in the paper recycling bin.

'Stories from now on will be commissioned,' said Yamparti. 'It will be better that way.'

Who was I to argue? At least we could walk on the floor without tripping on mounds of unread words.

'But how will we find new writers?' I asked.

'I know a richer and better source of writing,' said Yamparti. 'I know some wonderful writers from a writing group I'm in. I also know this one new writer. They're so highly regarded, Dibble and Bains have won the rights to publish his first novel, *Dreamtime in Suburbia*, and he wants to publish some of his short stories with us.'

'Who's the writer?' I asked, excited about publishing the next big thing.

'Ki Goonawanda, and he really wants to meet you, Charles. He knows of you.'

'Ki who?' I asked, scratching my head. 'I don't know anyone by that name.'

'There was a message via the magazine's email, requesting your contact details. He wants to set up a private meeting with you at the Young and Jackson,' explained Yamparti, her usually sour disposition dissolving into animated excitement. 'You should have told me you knew one of the most exciting new Indigenous voices in Australia.'

The initial surprise in knowing an actual up-and-coming author, who wanted to publish their works with my magazine, turned to shock when the Ki Goonawanda I found waiting for me in the Young and Jackson, sipping Cognac below Chloe, was none other than a fellow Victoria Grammarian. One I knew all too well.

'Some of the boys from school tell me you're loaded since your old man passed away, Casper. Sorry for your loss.'

Casper was my nickname all through my time at Victoria Grammar.

'Thanks, Brains,' I replied.

'With my father's rude health, I'll have to wait at least thirty years before I inherit the house on Lake Geneva and the London flat.'

'It's better to have parents alive, Brains,' I admitted.

'You were always the dreamy, sentimental type, Casper,' said Brains, or should I have called him by his nom de plume, Ki Goonawanda, or his real name, Eugene Whiteford.

Eugene was a year ahead of me at school; a bellowing sergeant major at Cadets, a prefect, and one of the top one hundred students in the state in his final year. His father was an international lawyer, academic, and advisor to various Labour governments around the world, who wrote three ponderous tomes on human rights, and Australia's failings against these lofty standards. By all accounts, Whiteford senior, by those who came across his path, was a large, imposing, intelligent pig of a human being, who sought to dominate lesser mortals through his size and intellect.

These self-same traits were evident in his son too. To his face, the younger boys called him 'Brains'. How Eugene loved that. But behind his back, the boys called him 'BASE', abbreviation for 'Biggest Almightiest Shit Ever'.

BASE, when not content to wow the teachers with his intellect, opining his thoughts from one school publication to another, loved nothing better than to belittle those inferior types like me who came across his path. He was the type of person who loved power, who loved even more wielding it, and simply purred with an indescribable joy on the discomfort and embarrassment his power caused. I was one of his favourite targets, one of those people whose heart sank every time he saw BASE come around the corner. Of course, BASE never understood his effect on others. As far as he was concerned, the sun shined out of his golden and beautifully formed posterior.

'Of course, I love my parents,' said Eugene. 'But it would be nice to come into my inheritance a little earlier. But while I wait, I'm forging my own way in life.'

'My editor, Yamparti, tells me you're quite the writer,' I said.

Eugene's podgy face broke into a self-satisfied grin. 'That's right, I've packed in the legal profession. After Victoria Grammar, I studied law at Melbourne uni. I hated every moment of it. Tedious subject: so tedious, I joined as many social groups as possible to relieve the boredom. One of them was a writing group. I loved it so much, I started to write fiction every moment I could. I was always good at bullshitting, and fiction is just the art of writing crap and making people believe it. Of course, I kept at my studies and passed with distinction. After uni I worked as an intellectual property lawyer. I groan even now thinking about those five awful years, catching the train, sitting at a desk, and reading the most tedious mind-numbing briefs. One morning, I woke up and thought I couldn't do this anymore, so I packed it all away and joined a squat in Collingwood and started writing full-time. Of course, between you and me, Casper,' said Eugene, leaning forward, 'the monthly allowance from the old man helps. I don't know what I would do without it. Although it's important to struggle, there's no point in struggling too much, if you know what I mean,' he said, chuckling.

'I'd like to read some of your writing,' I admitted.

'I'm giving two pieces to your magazine,' said Eugene. 'Of course, not my best work, you hear. I'm holding that back for another publication, and your editor said I'd be compensated. You see, Ki's work is starting to get noticed. Sally Diamond at Dibble and Bains says Ki's the next big thing. An Indigenous Hunter S. Thompson meets Peter Carey — not that I care about the comparison. I'll leave that for the critics to decide.' Eugene took a sip of his cognac and continued, 'Sally will be at the launch of your magazine next week. I'll introduce you to her. However, you need to keep the fact I'm Ki a secret. She thinks I'm Ki's literary agent. His white big brother. As far as she knows, Ki has abandoned Melbourne after ten years practising law, to be closer to his people in the Northern Territory. You'll keep it a secret. I'm invoking the old-school-tie code, of course.'

'Isn't what you're doing a tad unethical?'

'Not at all. I'm striking a blow for all Indigenous voices.'

I crossed my arms and frowned.

Eugene, obviously noting my scepticism, sighed and put down his cognac. 'Look, Casper, you must understand,' he continued. 'No one wants to publish a posh public schoolboy these days. You'll have a devil of a time getting anyone to take you seriously, unless you change your backstory and make it as exotic as possible. Then, people will be feting you as the next big thing.' Eugene took up his glass again and placed it to his lips but didn't drink. Instead, he gazed out into the room, appearing absent-minded. 'You and I, Casper,' said Eugene, 'and everything we represent — wealth, wasp power, and the old school tie — is now despised by the elites. They hate us, Casper, except the power they think we wield.' He took a long sip of his cognac and placed the glass back down on the table. 'Of course, we could complain about being on the bottom of their intersectionality hierarchy. We could try and fight back. But why? If you ask me, it's high time other races and groups took charge. That's why the nom de plume. If you can't beat 'em I say, join 'em.'

'It sounds like racism to me,' I said.

'That's where you're wrong,' said Eugene. 'What's happening is a long overdue readjustment, to right past injustices. For too long, people like you and me had it all. Now it's time to sit back and let all the marginalised groups run things.'

'Still sounds like racism and intolerance to me,' I said, shaking my head imperceptibly. 'Whatever happened to Martin Luther King's, "I have a dream" speech? Where a person should be judged by the content of their character and not the colour of their skin.'

'Really, Casper, you're too sentimental,' said Eugene, purring with mirth. 'Too naïve. No one on the left believes in tolerance and fairness. And these days, the left runs everything. The only thing the left cares about is power, and intersectionality is their way of maintaining control. Divide people into categories based on their immutable characteristics, then play one group off against another. Men against women. Blacks against whites. The poor against the rich and middle class. Everyone at each other's throats all the time.'

'I still think it's highly unethical of you to pretend to be Indigenous.'

'You should talk, with an editor named Yamparti,' snapped Eugene. 'What's the story with her?'

'She has Indigenous blood in her,' I stammered, suddenly returning to my schoolboy days, overwhelmed by the imposing figure of Eugene: prefect and one of the top students in the state.

'Really.' Eugene snorted. 'Or maybe she's another white girl trying to get ahead in a culture slanted against her.'

We fell silent for a time.

Eugene was right. Who was I to question him, pretending to be an Indigenous writer to get a book deal. Yet no matter how much I tried rationalising it, a nagging question remained. 'Don't Dibble and Bains realise that Ki is a hoax?' I blurted out. 'That a person like you is pretending to be an Indigenous writer?'

'Not at all. You see, Ki says all the right things.'

'What things?'

'There is a strong demand from publishers, agents and readers for new and exotic voices,' said Eugene. 'Not the same dreary white male authors, with their wasp-centric view of the world. Unfortunately, the quality of work of some of the newer voices is not quite there yet. Also, they're not hitting the right political notes. Most of the literary agents love the names, the colour of their skin, even their sexuality, but if only they could write better, and say the right things politically. That's why they love Ki so much and don't question his story. Not only does he tick all the right intersectional boxes, he also says all the right things, politically.' He leant back in his seat and took another swig of his cognac. 'That's what you should do, Casper. Change your name, create an alternate reality for yourself. Maybe start writing under a woman's name. Look at Mary Ann Evans. To have her writing taken seriously in Victorian England, she needed to start writing as George Eliot. You won't get published otherwise. To be a writer, Casper, you need to be ruthless.'

We fell silent.

I gazed at my beer. When I lifted my eyes, I found Eugene staring at me over the rim of his glass.

'I didn't believe it at first when I found out *the* Charles Western, I knew from Victoria Grammar, was behind a new literary magazine.'

'Well, I've set one up,' I said, blushing and feeling uncomfortable under the steady gaze of Eugene.

Eugene took another sip of his cognac. Then shifting back in his seat and swilling his glass, he continued to consider me — as if I was some amusing moth or snail from a biology class assignment — one eyebrow raised, a wry smile creasing his face. 'You were always a funny fellow, Casper. You do know why we called you Casper, don't you?'

'My blonde hair and fair skin: like a ghost?'

'It was more than that. It was as if you were a spectre from an unearthly plane. You always seemed to be a million miles away. Some of the boys thought you were from another planet, beaming into Earth. That's why they all mercilessly picked on you at school. The Form Masters could never get through to you.' Eugene frowned intently at me before continuing, 'I often saw you walking around the oval by yourself at lunch time or sitting alone in the library, staring into space. What went through your mind? School work wasn't one of them, clearly. I heard from a few old boys that you failed your VCE.'

'I didn't study well that year.' Heat was once again engulfing my head, and now beads of sweat fell from my hairline.

'What happened?' Eugene was no longer the jovial yet cynical soul explaining the Ki Goonawanda hoax, but a frowning, critical, older boy upset by a younger boy letting down the House.

'I don't know,' I admitted.

'Come now, you must have been thinking of something.'

'I don't know,' I stammered.

'I heard you walked out in the middle of your VCE English exam. Why?'

I dropped my head.

'I also heard you had a job working in a hotel but was sacked. You left the freezer door open and let all the stock defrost. News does travel, you know, Casper.' The smug smile I knew so well, the taunting eyes, the cruel face from school had returned.

I leapt to my feet. 'I'm late for dinner with my nan,' I said, saying the first thing that popped into my head. 'Nice to see you again, Brains.'

'Don't take it the wrong way, Casper. I'm not having a go at you,' said

Eugene, jumping to his feet also. 'I just want to know what goes through that head of yours … What made you think of creating a magazine? You didn't even pass English.'

I looked at Chloe, lost momentarily for words. 'I don't know why,' I said after a time. 'Maybe I wanted to create my own business.' I hated myself at that moment. As if I had reached inside myself and found no reason except the most hackneyed one. I turned and walked away.

I made it as far as the stairs when Eugene called out, 'Remember to keep our little secret,' he said. 'Old school tie and all.'

'Of course,' I said, feeling once more a timid and bullied fourteen-year-old boy in the presence of the brilliant and up-and-coming prefect and straight-A student. I turned and took the stairs.

As I reached the bottom step, Eugene cried out, 'Casper!'

I turned and looked up.

Eugene stood at the top of the stairs, with his glass raised. 'To literature! May it make us rich and infamous.'

I gave a weak smile before continuing out into the clear night air. Swanston Street was pulsating with the footfall of nine-to-five workers, and the *rat tat tat* of pedestrian crossings. I dashed across Flinders Street to the station, losing myself in a crush of pedestrians, trying to put as much distance between myself and Brains.

CHAPTER 11

Career Advice

You remember it so well, don't you, Charles — I told myself. That hour trapped inside Mr Drummond's office. You thought you could forget it, and for a long time you succeeded, burying it down, deep down in a coffin marked 'forget'. But now after your meeting with Brains, it claws its way up from the grave, grabbing hold of your attention, sucking the joy from your life …

You're in year ten. Outside, the spring sun shines upon the school, but in Mr Drummond's office, it is so dark and cold, you shiver in the chair. You're terrified of Mr Drummond's hairy fingers, gripping Dr Regi's report. You close your eyes and listen to Mr Drummond's wristwatch marking time. You take a deep breath, scared your heart might gallop ahead of the seconds and minutes of your life, becoming dissected upon the chopping board of time. Outside, Eugene's voice hollers an order to the cadets, and the crunch of steel-capped boots on asphalt begins.

Finally, your Form Master's bald head emerges from Dr Regi's psychiatric assessment and sighs. How that face never fails to scare you. And if you're still honest with yourself, Charles, that bald-headed skull, those piercing black peppercorn eyes still scare you, still catapult you from your sleep. Whenever you shudder to think of him, he reminds you of a dark sinister raven upon a tombstone. A tombstone signifying the grave holding all your dreams, hopes and happiness.

You sit there stupidly trying to imagine Mr Drummond as a boy like you. What boy — when confronted with questions about his fitness for school, questions about his sanity, even his fitness for a normal life — sits and thinks these thoughts?

Not other boys. Just you, Charles. Stupid, empty-headed Charles, with nothing better to do than consider whether your Form Master was a boy like you. You can't see how it would be possible. Instead, you see him already fully formed: his cranium pulsating with mathematical formulas.

'The Raven' takes off his glasses and leans back in his leather armchair. It squeaks and groans, as if he's squashing doves. He seems to be considering you closely. 'Western, we are all concerned about you,' he finally says, resettling his glasses and bolting up right in his chair with a snap, as if coming to a definite opinion and needing to articulate it as quickly and hurriedly as possible. 'We don't like to fail any student,' he says. 'We also understand you have issues, and we want to ensure you get the best care possible. But we need to know why you left the European History exam without writing a word. Mr Davis says you're one of his best students.'

As the ineffectual creature that you are, you drop your head. You don't say anything. Instead, you blush like a coward. How silly you look. How silly you feel. What a waste of space.

'Why?' the Raven repeats.

'I don't know why, sir. Dr Regi says I like to self-sabotage.'

The Raven exhales and leans back in his chair frowning. It squeaks as if he smothers a mouse with his large frame. He considers you closely for a time over the rims of his glasses, before he picks up the report again. 'I read that. But we don't need to be defined by reports or psychological assessments, Western. As long as you take your medication and try to capture your thoughts before they get out of control, there is no reason why you shouldn't live a healthy productive life.'

'Yes, sir.'

'What do you want to do with yourself, Western?' Those sharp eyes fix on you, as pins would pierce a dead moth to a display board.

'Leave this office, sir.'

You smirk. You're not funny. You don't mean it to be funny. You're a small, insignificant creature, who doesn't know why he has said it. You say it out of embarrassment.

'Don't be silly, Western,' barks Drummond. 'What do you want to do with your life?'

'What do I want to do?' you repeat, dazed, uncertain whether you can say it.

The crunching cadet boots come to a halt outside the window. A currawong in the bright spring sunshine warbles a tune. The grounds keeper's mower hums. The curtain flutters, bringing with it the scent of the garden and cut grass.

'Well, Western, what do you want to do with your life?' your Form Master repeats. These words echo in your mind and demand an answer; the Raven's eyes examining you like some obtuse mathematical problem.

You hesitate at first.

Then you take a deep breath and blow out the answer weakly.

'I want to be a writer.'

The Raven leans forward. 'You want to be a waiter?'

'No, a writer,' you repeat louder.

'A writer,' he gasps. His tiny eyes widen. The veins in his hairless head pulsate. He looks genuinely shocked, even puzzled, as if stumped by an unexpected chess move. 'A writer, eh.' He considers this for a time. 'What type of writer?'

'A fiction writer,' you say nervously, as if you have said the wrong thing and now want to take it all back.

'What are your marks like in English.'

'I don't know, sir.'

You do know, but like the stupid and dumb person you are, you can't remember them. At the first sign of pressure, any pressure, thoughts abandon your mind, like rats from a sinking and rotting ship.

'From what Mr Rivers tells me, not too good.' The Raven gives you a quick and disapproving glance before he leans back in his leather armchair and opines: 'It was George Bernard Shaw, I believe, who said that to become a writer, you must spend twenty years in the British Museum writing. Doesn't matter whether your wife and family are starving, you keep writing, and after twenty years, you throw all your work away and start again. Are you prepared to do the same, Western?'

'I don't know, sir.' Your mind is now drifting away. You dream of a flying house hovering over a lake.

'You don't want to be a writer,' he says. 'Frankly, with your marks, you wouldn't be a good author. What you need to do is look at a practical profession. Something that can keep you from your overactive imagination …'

Eugene's voice starts hollering orders, and those polished and hardened boots begin stomping in unison. They drown out Mr Drummond's voice as they march through my consciousness, flattening every thought in their path, crushing this memory that spirals down, down into the subconscious.

You're nothing, nothing, nothing.

Eugene was right. I had failed at everything I did. I flunked my final year at Victoria Grammar. Failing English. Failing English! While other students read the prescribed texts — *1984*, *To Kill a Mockingbird*, *My Brother Jack*, *The Great Gatsby* — I read *Remembrance of Things Past*, *The Tibetan Book of the Dead*, *The Library of Babel*. The more obscure the text the better. I ditched all the prescribed texts for my other subjects as well, for my own eccentric reading list: Christian mysticism, French existentialists. I soon took to writing.

The common refrain on my personality?

Too impractical, one Master wrote in a report card.

His head is in the clouds, another one wrote.

Bright, another said, *but he doesn't want to concentrate.*

After flunking out of school, I worked in the five-star hotel Eugene spoke about. And yes, I was sacked after leaving the freezer door open. It was one of the last in a series of self-inflicted blunders.

After my father died, his company offered me a job in one of his stores. 'Carry on your father's legacy,' one of the directors said.

'I want to forge my own way in life,' I had told him.

A convenient lie.

I didn't trust myself to succeed. Instead, I worked in a menswear store in the city, until my daydreaming became so intense that I failed to serve any customers. They let me go after two months. I worked in a restaurant for a time, but the grind of serving demanding customers proved too much, and after pouring hot soup over an obnoxious diner, they also let me go.

Each job started with hope and ended with failure and a quick dismissal.

After procrastinating for several months, I enrolled in an Accountancy TAFE course. Why accountancy? It was a practical course the Raven would have approved of. Yet after paying for the course and buying the prescribed textbooks, I failed to attend a class, or read any of the source material.

I then worked in a bookstore in Brunswick for a few months. One of those dimly lit stores buried in an obscure laneway. I loved the job. The way it afforded me time to think, to daydream. I loved all those obscure books on the shelves waiting to be discovered, the smell of the paper, and the whispered quietness of the moth-eaten customers. I loved the job so much, I walked out — never to return.

'Why? Why? Why?' I once asked while shaking my head in Dr Regi's office during one of our sessions.

So, dear reader, you might be wondering what I liked to do with my time? From my earliest childhood, I liked nothing better than lying down in a patch of grass, and staring up into the sky, weaving fantastical stories in my imagination.

As a young boy, I played the role of a soldier sent off to fight the Japanese in the hills of New Guinea, single-handedly stopping an entire army from taking Port Moresby. For a time, I became a policeman fighting crime on an industrial scale. In another, I was a spy, foiling Russian and Chinese plots left, right and centre. These daydreams, fuelled from my incessant reading, became more sophisticated and more fantastical as I turned into a teenager, then a young man.

In a fantasy that occupied two years, I had built an army of flying robots that fought an imaginary war with another likeminded but evil boy in Geelong — our crafts crisscrossing Port Phillip Bay to attack each other's bases. We had watercraft, fashioned in the image of Luke Skywalker's T-65 X-wing starfighter, fighting on the water.

In another daydream, which I spun out for a year, I built a colony in the middle of the Simpson Desert, fusing Indigenous culture with Western art and science. How this colony attracted all the great minds of the world.

This dream soon morphed into me playing the character of a brilliant scientist, revolutionising our understanding of quantum physics. In one brilliant paper, this scientist laid out a radical rethink of gravity; postulating laws that allowed humans to escape the Earth's gravitational field with little energy, and thereby gifting humans the chance to spread out across the cosmos. As this scientist, I lived in a remote mountain mansion by a lake, tucked in an extra-dimensional pocket, where twenty-four hours in the property were only one hour in the real world. Here, living alone, I read books and smoked cigars, writing out my theories. My inspiration derived from the aliens who visited occasionally to hand down their cosmic secrets.

As I matured and discovered the opposite sex and the heartache of loving unattainable girls, I developed a story about being the losing point of a love triangle. This daydream induced months of morbid self-pity, and I soon abandoned it for a tale of revenge, after reading *The Count of Monte Cristo.*

In another daydream, I became a future Australian prime minister of French descent who stood up to the aggressions of the Chinese. In a war, the Australian Army defeated an alliance of the Chinese, Russians, and Iranians, establishing a Southeast Asian zone of influence, stretching from the Antarctica to Hong Kong.

These daydreams — which I incessantly brooded on from the moment I woke, till the time I went to sleep — were my refuge from a world of bullying and loneliness.

Then came Melbourne's never-ending lockdown.

I decided to use this time to become a writer. I purchased twenty 500-page-lined notebooks, fifty ballpoint pens, a laptop and locked myself in my flat, determined — like my hero, Marcel Proust — to sleep by day and write by night, spinning an intricate three-hundred-thousand-word novel based on one of my fantastical daydreams.

After reading *A Moveable Feast,* by Hemmingway, in my first week of isolation, I even bought a case of white rum, with the intention of drinking a Hemmingway Daiquiri each night as I hardened my whimsical fantasies into solid and true stories. In my first notebook entry, which I fantasised future generations would read, I declared my aim was to fuse the style of Hemmingway with Proust. I would write one true sentence, which went on and on and on.

Yet, the more I tried to write, the more I procrastinated.

The fantastical imaginings, which all through my childhood and teenage years had kept me company and content, on the page seemed limpid and stupid, idiotic and without any vitality.

I then realised my stories only made sense to me. I had nothing to say. Nothing to write. I was such a failure.

After only one hour of writing, I fell into bad habits, drinking rum and ordering ridiculous items from eBay. My flat quickly overflowing with quidditch sticks, Tibetan healing sound bowls, an Indian wigwam, and a digeridoo.

Finally, during a break in lockdown, Nan put an end to my Proustian living arrangements.

'Oh my god,' she said, stiffening and wincing in the doorway. I had never heard her invoke the deity outside of church before. 'Look at this mess.' Nan stared open-mouthed at the floor that was covered in empty rum bottles and Menulog bags, plus pizza boxes with half-eaten and mouldy crusts still inside. 'And that smell,' she cried, grabbing her nose. 'It's so strong it should be paying *you* rent.'

I'm sorry, Nan, I'm such a failure — I wanted to say, but I didn't. Instead, I looked around at my own filth.

'Either you look for work, Charles, or I'll move in with you,' she said after we cleaned up.

Once the lockdown eased, I ran away to Europe, and that's when I had my epiphany below *The Last Supper.*

I was nothing more than a failure. This magazine would no doubt fail. I failed at everything I did. What was the point of trying?

CHAPTER 12

Magazine Launch

A teaspoon on an empty champagne flute gave out five discordant high-pitched dings. The babbling in the packed Young and Jackson subsided into silence.

'Friends,' said Yamparti, standing on a chair in the middle of the room. 'Thank you all for coming to this auspicious event: the birth of a new literary magazine. First, however, I'd like to begin by acknowledging the traditional owners and custodians of the land on which we meet today, the peoples of the Kulin nation. I also pay my respects to their elders past and present. I would also like to acknowledge Sally Diamond, from Dibble and Bains, as well as representatives from Federal and State Labor.' Yamparti paused and scanned the assembled throng before continuing, 'I'm so proud to be the editor of *Imagine*. It's not often you get to be involved in something at the beginning. *Imagine* will be used as a vehicle to promote tolerance and diversity, as well as nurturing new and exciting literary talent. I'm pleased to announce that *Imagine* will feature the works of the up-and-coming Indigenous writer, Ki Goonawanda. Unfortunately, he cannot be here this evening.' A brief smile flittered across her face before she resumed her speech. '*Imagine* will be about nurturing new and original voices, like Ki's. About giving a voice to the voiceless, of seeking to help the marginalised and oppressed. It will also fight the reactionary right-wing forces in Canberra and Washington. Friends, I thank you for being here at the birth of this new magazine. Now, drink up.'

The room erupted with applause.

I clapped too, then nudged Nan, who was sitting next to me on the sofa. 'Well, what do you think?' I said, lifting my voice to be heard over the cacophony of voices resuming their chatter.

'She didn't mention my grandson in her speech. It's *your* magazine, she should have mentioned that,' replied Nan, frowning.

'I didn't ask her to mention me.'

'Well, she should have mentioned you. Besides, you should have been the one to give the speech.'

'I told you I don't like to speak in public.'

'You shouldn't let that incident in sixth grade define the rest of your life. I thought you spoke to Dr Regi about it?'

I reddened.

We fell silent for a time — Nan watching Yamparti, who was a little way off, surrounded by her university mates; while I scanned the crowd, a little disappointed ... Celeste hadn't come. I had left an invitation for her with another librarian rostered on, not having the courage to invite her myself.

'Your friend has an interesting dress sense,' said Nan, still looking at Yamparti.

'All the girls at university dress like that.'

'Well, I think her nose stud and apricot hair a very daring look.'

'Don't be so judgemental, Nan,' I said.

'I'm not being judgemental,' she said. 'I'm being complimentary. Girls in my day would never have the confidence to dye their hair the colour of a bathroom wall.'

'Nan.'

'I'm being complimentary, Charles. Truly, I am. As for her name Yam ... Yampart ...'

'Yamparti,' I corrected.

'Yamparti. Is it Portuguese?'

'No, she's part Aboriginal.'

'It must be a very tiny part,' said Nan, pursing her lips.

'Her grandmother was Indigenous.'

'She doesn't look Aboriginal. She looks Welsh.'

'I didn't know the Welsh had apricot hair.' I laughed.

'They don't, dear, but I can always tell where a person is from. It's one of my special powers. Scratch the surface and you'll find she's a middle-class girl from a Welsh family. What's her last name?'

'Jones.'

'Ah, you see,' said Nan.

'Casper!' Out of the crush of people, Eugene appeared, and grabbing me by the wrist, he lifted me to my feet.

I was glad of the interruption. Nan's negativity was beginning to sour my evening.

'I want you to meet Sally, from Dibble and Bains,' said Eugene, dragging me through a knot of people. 'Sally, this is Charles Western, the owner of the magazine.'

Sally, a small, petite woman with long dark hair, fixed me with her expressive eyes, as if I was a sociological experiment gone horribly wrong. She nodded imperceptibly to acknowledge my presence before her eyes shot back to Eugene. 'When are you going to introduce me to Ki? We're all desperate to meet him, at D and B.'

'He's shy and doesn't do social,' said Eugene, giving me a momentary wink. 'Besides, he's busy writing a follow-up to *Dreamtime in Suburbia*.'

'Well, you tell him from us, we are all desperate to meet him.'

'I was thinking, Sally,' said Eugene. 'As you liked *Dreamtime in Suburbia* so much, I could offer you a similar novel, one I'm working on at present. Ki likes it, and I think it would fit right in with your roster of books.'

'I've always liked your work, Eugene. Why don't you send it to my email: Sally dot diamond at Dibble Bains, all one word in lowercase, dot com.'

Eugene took out his pen and notebook and scribbled this down.

'You know, Sally, Charles here is a writer himself,' said Eugene, snapping shut his notebook. 'He wrote one of the stories in the first edition, *Waiting*.'

Sally Diamond frowned. 'Yes, I did read that story. I found it … I found it interesting.'

'Sally Diamond.' Karen, appearing out of the crush of people, pushed past me to stand only inches from Sally, who took a step back in obvious alarm. 'I'm so glad to have this opportunity to talk to you in person,' said Karen, stepping into Sally's space once more. 'I have a number of works I know you'd just love.'

'At the moment, we're not taking any more submissions,' replied Sally, stepping back again.

'But if I could take a few minutes of your time, to show you how Dibble and Bains could profit from publishing my works …'

Sally Diamond walked away.

Karen, clearly not to be deterred, followed in pursuit.

Soon they were lost in the crowd, with Eugene trailing after them.

I hunted for Nan in the room, finding her spot on the sofa empty.

Finally, I gave up, and having no one to talk to, I latched onto the first person I came across: a burly middle-aged man holding a stubby of craft beer. With his ironed flannelette shirt and pressed khaki pants, he looked so out of place surrounded by the grungy, hip attire of the wannabe Melbourne literary set.

'You must be Barry,' I said, finally connecting the bald head, the grizzled beard, to Karen's depiction of her husband in *Under a Samoan*

Sky. 'I'm Charles Western.'

He shook my hand, and I felt my face heat up. What would I speak to Barry about now, as we watched Karen chase Sally Diamond about the room? Should I say: 'How's the chemo?' Or maybe: 'Your wife told me all about her affair on the cruise. I bet you're pissed about that?'

Thankfully, Barry spoke first, 'You don't know what the footy score is, by the way? My mobile's flat.'

'No, sorry,' I said. 'I don't even know who's playing. But I think it's on the screen in the next room.'

'Thanks, but I'd rather be at home with my feet up watching it on the telly. This might be Karen's scene, but it certainly isn't mine.'

'Have you read any of her stories?' I asked.

'Tried to read one book she gave me, *Under a Samoan Sky*. Don't tell Karen, but I couldn't make head or tail of it.'

'You didn't recognise anyone in the book?'

'No, should I have?'

'No. No,' I said, blushing again.

We fell silent as we both watched the people in the room talking and laughing.

I racked my brain for a less awkward topic. 'I bet you miss work?' I said, landing on this thread after a few minutes of uncomfortable silence.

'Pardon?' said Barry.

'Um, how you're not working at the moment.'

His frowning incomprehension made me flush again. I really wasn't good with small talk. I kept putting my foot in it.

'What has Karen been saying?' he queried, turning all his 200-centimetre, 110-kilogram frame to face me.

'Um, that you can't work because of your cancer.'

'I only missed six weeks early last year,' spat Barry. 'That's all. Worked straight through and am still working.'

'Charles!' Boris stepped out of the crowd, and taking me by the arm, he led me away from Barry.

I'd never been gladder to see Boris in all my life.

'Did you hear that speech she gave?' he whispered. 'She didn't mention us once. Not once. You see what she's doing, boss? Squeezing us out. You need to do something before she turns the magazine into a home for all her hairy-legged feminist friends.'

'Relax, everything is under control,' I said. 'I've spoken to Yamparti, and we came to an agreement that there won't be any more overt political essays.'

'You're too trusting, boss. She's taking advantage of you.' Boris clutched my arm tighter. 'Well, have you thought any more about our business proposition?'

'I'm still thinking it through—'

'Charles?' Nan appeared at my side, putting on her gloves.

I felt like one of those participants in a Jane Austen movie dance scene, moving methodically from one dance partner to the next, just as the conversation turned awkward. I really didn't want to tell Boris I wasn't interested in his proposal. I didn't have the heart or stomach, or the bravery.

'It's time I left,' she said.

'Won't you stay a little longer?'

'I don't know anyone.'

'Let me introduce you to my friends.'

'It's late, Charles.'

'Let me walk you to a cab, then.'

'I hope you had a good time?' I asked as a blast of cool but clean evening air washed over us when we stepped out onto the street.

'I did, Charles. I did,' she said while I hailed a cab on the corner of Swanston and Flinders.'

'Do you like the magazine?'

'I'm happy for you, Charles, very happy for you,' she said in a flat tone as a cab pulled alongside.

'They're my friends, Nan.'

'I know, dear. I know they are, but you will promise me one thing. You will see my accountant, Terry Smith, first thing on Monday?'

'Nan, I've told you I'm careful with my money.'

'Is this magazine leading anywhere?'

'Making money is not the only thing in life,' I said.

'I know, but I don't want people taking advantage of my grandson. You're too trusting and—'

'My friends wouldn't do anything to let me down,' I said, cutting her off before she said it out loud.

'Of course, but please let Terry look at the financial side of the magazine, for my sake.'

'You better go, Nan.' I opened the cab door and helped her in.

'You haven't answered my question, Charles!' said Nan through the backseat window.

'Go,' I said to the driver.

The cab sped away, Nan's head poking out of the back-seat window. 'You haven't answered my question!' she cried.

The cab was speeding across Princess Bridge by the time I thought of answering, and by then it was too late.

CHAPTER 13

MY FRIEND SAM

I couldn't believe it! I held in my hands the magazine. The inspiration I extracted from *The Last Supper* and carried with me all through my European sojourn was now ink and paper, coursing through the literary avenues of the city. All weekend, I read and re-read every article and short story, with a particular focus on my work. I winced at some of my purplier patches and determined to write better.

On Saturday afternoon, I went to the State Library, and with no Celeste on duty, I left a copy of the magazine for her with another librarian, attaching a note: *The first edition of my magazine for the loveliest of all librarians in Melbourne. Yours always, Charles.*

On Sunday, I wrote another story. It came quickly, and it seemed to write itself. It was about a man, named Oberon, who was living one hundred years in the future; he was to be executed, with no reason given, and he ignored the impending doom until it was too late. The guards imprisoned him in his house, and in the minutes leading up to his death, Oberon pleaded with a priest, Brother Thomas, from the dominant religion — a New Age cult — for release. A debate between Oberon and Brother Thomas was to follow, until resigned to his fate, Oberon was led to his death.

All day I wrote the story, driven on by the inspiration of the magazine. If I worked hard, I could have it ready for the second edition. By Sunday night, it was done, and I emailed it to my new friends, with a note for them to read it and let me know what they thought. I practically ran down St Kilda Road on Monday morning, such was my excitement to hear their opinion.

As I exited the elevator on the floor of the office, I heard my name. I stopped and looked up. It came from the office, which had the door wide open. It wasn't directed at me but was Yamparti's voice.

'Did you read Charles' latest story?' asked Yamparti.

'About the guy called Oberon,' said Boris. 'Complete crap, like his stupid story in the magazine, *Waiting*.'

'What, worse than *Waiting*?' Karen replied with a laugh.

'*Waiting*, what a terrible story.' Yamparti snorted.

'I couldn't *wait* to finish it!' said Boris.

They all cackled.

'I was talking to someone who went to school with him, at the launch, Eugene Whiteford. He said he has serious mummy issues,' Yamparti added, chuckling.

They all giggled.

'I feel embarrassed publishing it at all,' said Yamparti. 'Eugene has warned me not to publish his writing. Ki Goonawanda might not want to associate his works with Charles' immature stories. But what can I do? He's the owner.'

'He doesn't have any talent for writing, that's for sure,' said Karen.

'Or a head for a magazine,' added Yamparti.

'If it wasn't for the money,' said Boris. 'I wouldn't work here.'

'Or me,' said Karen.

'Look,' said Boris in a serious voice, 'we must stop fighting among ourselves and work together. Charlie boy might have the money, but he doesn't have a clue about writing, running a business, or anything in between.'

'Agreed,' said Yamparti.

'We need to stick together,' continued Boris. 'The three of us decide on what to do, then we tell Charles.'

'Charles is easily led,' said Karen. 'He'll do what we tell him, but we need to be united.'

'Agreed,' said Yamparti.

I suppose, dear reader, you want to know what I felt in those hours after tiptoeing away from the office. No doubt you want me, like a novelist describing an emotional crisis of a heroine, to lay bare the intricate details of my feelings, explain them all from a thousand different and sometimes contradictory angles. Discard the plot of my story for a time, to revel in my inner turmoil. Or failing that, with a few deft strokes of my pen, dissect my soul upon the page for you to titter and laugh at.

Well, no. I'll not do that.

It's not that I refuse. Or that I want to shake my fist at you, for your voyeurism. I've been laughed at all my life. Nor is it from any modesty that I refrain from doing so. If I have learnt one thing from Karen Tiven, it is that all writing is autobiographical; and as a writer (a poor, purple-patched, hopeless, cliché-ridden writer at that), I'm willing to sacrifice everything: family, friends, even my feelings — miserable and unimportant as they are — to the greatest cause of all: fiction.

No.

The reason I can't describe my thoughts and feelings, is that I don't have any. Or any I can identify and describe.

At that time, I walked numbly and aimlessly around the city in the pouring rain. I remember nothing, save for a few discordant images. The crushed cigarette packet I squelched under foot; the upturned rubbish bin; the dirty puddles in a deserted lane; the sight of a dead seagull in a gutter; ants feeding upon its spilt entrails; the smell of carbon monoxide and dog shit.

I was conscious of the rain falling, falling, and my clothes becoming wetter and wetter: my shoes beginning to squelch, my teeth beginning to chatter. I had nowhere to go, yet no reason to stop. I might possibly have kept going around and around the city ... except, on Princess Bridge, a voice stopped me.

'Salvation is at hand?' A little lady, hooded in a yellow raincoat, walked towards me.

I could ignore the stares of the self-absorbed pedestrians I passed; I just sidestepped them and kept walking. But the look of compassion in this woman's eyes brought tears to mine. They ran down my cheeks. Thankfully, they were obscured by the rain falling from my hair and down my face.

'The Lord is here to help you.' She handed me a pamphlet titled: *Lord as Friend and Saviour*, with the picture of Jesus, arms outstretched, ready to embrace me with his love.

'I'm fine,' I said. 'In fact, I've never felt better. You see ... I'm waiting for someone to come. A friend. He's my saviour.'

'There is only one saviour ...' she began, but I lost her voice in the sound of slowed traffic running through puddles.

I gazed over the railing at the fast-flowing muddy water of the Yarra River. I could sense the woman standing next to me. I could feel her eyes studying me intently and thinking: another soul for salvation, another notch on her bible. I didn't want to give her the satisfaction. So, I waited for her to go.

Then, finally, she shouted, 'We're in Bourke Street, if you need us.'

I was alone now. I didn't need anyone. An insignificant miserable person such as me, wasn't needed by anyone. If it wasn't for the money, nobody would care if I lived or died.

Better to jump, I thought as I stared mesmerised at the fast-flowing water.

I may have climbed onto the railing, except *he* appeared in the corner of my eye. At first, he was a blur, yet through the tears and rain, he grew more distinct, and I grew more curious.

He looked like me. Or at least the *me* I thought myself to be, when I gazed into the mirror or thought about myself in the third person, in warmer, more positive moments. Except this double had thicker, fairer hair, not likely to turn into the balding palette Nan said awaited my skull in a few years. He was also taller, more athletic, with a tanned face and relaxed expression. He also had azure eyes. But unlike mine, they twinkled with vitality and optimism.

'What's happening, Charlie Boy?' said my double as he sidled up to me at the bridge railing and threw his arm over my shoulder like a long-lost friend; his twinkling eyes suggested mischief with every word.

'How do you know my name?' I asked.

'Let's just say I've been watching over you. I'm your guardian angel, as it were.'

'What's your name?' I asked.

'Why bother with names,' said my mysterious double. *'Some of us are what we are, regardless of a name, and others like me are what others make them to be. So, choose a name and make me as you will.'*

Although I considered his reasoning crazy and fatuous, a profound ring to his words, like a Pythagoras chord, vibrated within my soul. 'Sam. I'll call you Sam.'

'Sam it will be,' he said, lifting his head and laughing as the rain poured down. *'Sam it will be.'*

We shook hands then hugged like long-lost friends.

To those passing by car along the bridge, it must have been a curious sight. A young man in the pouring rain, wet to the core, with jerky hand movements. Another schizophrenic hobo? A performance artist perhaps? Looking back, I wonder if they saw Sam standing next to me at all. Saw his boisterous face, his arm around my shoulder. And if they didn't see him, whose fault would that be?

'I hear you need someone to manage a new magazine.'

'How do you know that?'

'I told you; I've been interested in your progress for many, many years.'

'Do you think you can do it?'

'What's that?'

'Run my magazine?'

'Can I do it,' Sam replied with a laugh. *'Why, you will find I have all the attributes needed.'*

We smiled, and then arm in arm, we walked back towards the office. We drew many stares as we strode down Swanston Street. I imagined what they saw: Sam — tall, tanned, athletic — with his arm over his smaller brother's shoulder, who was soaked to the core, shivering, his shoes squelching with each step.

'For your new position, Sam, you'll need a new suit and a haircut,' I suggested. 'New clothes — new person, as Nan always says.' I took Sam into the nearest available suit shop.

The shop assistant, a musty fossil of a man, at first tried to shoo me away. I might have fled embarrassed, except Sam whipped out my Mastercard, and the shop assistant's sniffy snoot dissolved into a courteous and servile smile.

'Don't fuss over me,' I said, staring into the mirror. 'It's Sam who needs the suit and the towel.'

'Of course, sir, whatever you say, sir,' he said, readjusting the hem of my trousers.

Finally, dry and out of my wet clothes, I bought a pair of 300-dollar leather Italian shoes for Sam and organised his haircut. After adjusting his gold- and white-striped silk tie, we stepped across the cobbled lane to the office.

The mouths of my subordinates were suitably ajar as I introduced Sam, no doubt impressed with his suit, Italian shoes, and his fifty-dollar haircut.

A puzzled look creased Yamparti's brow when I explained his new position. 'As of now,' I said after the introductions, 'I'll be taking a backseat while Sam runs the magazine. So, without further ado, I give you Sam.' I stepped back as Sam stepped forward, buttoning up his double-breasted suit.

'Good afternoon, colleagues, today a new broom is sweeping through the magazine. The old order is dead, and a new one takes its place. So, with that, I ask you all to go downstairs and stand on the footpath below the windows.'

The others looked at each other. The same look of perplexion when I first introduced Sam was creasing their brows.

'You heard me. Down on the street. NOW!'

'What's this all about—' Yamparti began.

'Downstairs, if you want to be paid this week!' shouted Sam. He had a booming voice when he wanted to make his point. It thrilled me to see the others scurrying out of the office.

'What are you going to do now?' I asked Sam.

'Just wait, Charlie boy.' Sam smiled. 'Just you wait and see.'

I had never been on the roof before, until led there by Sam. I was afraid of heights, but not Sam. He would dangle his legs over a fifty-storey building if needed. It was still pouring with rain as we looked over the edge and saw our three employees standing in a conspiratorial knot on the footpath below.

I guessed Sam's intention as I unfurled the umbrella I bought with the suit. Bob Hope did something similar to his script writers. Every payday, Bob Hope stood at the top of his mansion's staircase. Turning their pay cheques into paper airplanes, he launched them down at his script writers assembled at the foot of his stairs. 'The only exercise they ever got,' the King of Vaudeville quipped.

Boris looked like he needed a run.

From my jacket pocket, Sam took out their pay cheques.

I loved the idea of the chequebook and giving over cheques. I remembered my father's one as a small child, and when I finally came into money, I organised one to pay staff. Something about writing out the pays brought me closer to my father. Made me feel like a real businessman.

I held the umbrella aloft as Sam dangled the cheques over the edge.

'Hey, you down there! Do you want your pay?'

Not only did Boris, Karen and Yamparti look up, but half of the people gracing Flinders Lane also stopped to gaze up in my direction.

'Karen, you're first,' shouted Sam, dangling her cheque, then letting it go.

It tumbled in the rain and wind down Flinders Lane.

Karen, following it, bumped into annoyed pedestrians, parked cars, rubbish bins, and poles as she tried to keep beneath the drop zone.

Sam let go of Yamparti's, then Boris' cheques and watched them scurry down Flinders Lane.

'The guy on the roof is giving away money,' said someone.

'He might be going to jump,' said another.

A knot of people gathered on the street below. Many more curious onlookers came out onto the Lane.

'I've dropped three cheques, and those people are trying to steal them,' Sam cried down at them. 'You must help me.'

Never underestimate either the greed or the willingness of people to help others in genuine need. A disparate group of people below surged towards the three drop zones as the cheques fluttered, like descending dragonflies, in the rain and howling wind.

Sam and I then returned to the office, placed our feet on our desk and waited and waited and waited for the others to return.

A constable from Melbourne CIB eventually called. 'Do you know a Boris Petrović? He claims to work for you.'

'Boris Petrović … Boris Petrović,' Sam repeated, obviously mulling the name over in his mind. 'No, can't say I do. Wait a minute,' he cried before pausing for dramatic effect, no doubt, and seeming to consider a spot on the wall. 'No, sorry, I was thinking of another person. Why, what seems to be the problem officer?'

The policeman was reluctant to elaborate, suffice to say it was connected to a scuffle on the corner of Elizabeth Street and Flinders Lane, over a cheque.

'Terrible,' Sam said. 'Thank god for you boys in blue.'

The phone conversation ended. No doubt we would hear more about this incident later.

Yamparti returned a few minutes later, scratches across her face, her clothes and hair wet. She pointed her finger at me and screamed, 'At the last election, we voted to get rid of bastard bosses like you.'

'How do you know you didn't vote them in,' said Sam, smiling politely.

I was impressed with his comeback. I always struggled for a quick retort, too scared most times to say anything. But not Sam. Sam was quick-witted.

'This isn't the last you will hear about this. I'll take this further,' she added before storming out the door.

Fifteen minutes later, Karen arrived looking like a Scottish sheep dog with her soaked clothes and mattered hair. 'I've never been so humiliated in all my life,' she sobbed. 'I was set upon by three people.'

'Terrible,' said Sam. 'Simply dreadful.'

'I come here to do a job,' continued Karen, 'and all I get is abuse from Yamparti, and now I'm set upon by a mob. The look in their eyes … They wanted to kill me!' She burst into tears.

'Consider it good for your writing,' said Sam. 'You can use the incident in one of your novels or short stories.'

'Charles, Sam is mad.'

'Charles is not in charge,' said Sam. 'I am.'

'I want Charles back.' Karen sniffed. 'He was so sweet.'

'Sweet is out. Mean and daring is in. Now come on, Charles,' said Sam, taking his feet off the desk. 'Let me show you how much more attractive and magnetic I am.'

'Charles, are you okay?' asked Karen in a timid voice.

'I'm wonderful, Miss Tiven. Now, if you'll excuse me, Sam wants me to follow him.'

CHAPTER 14

SWEEPING A LIBRARIAN
OFF HER FEET

Sam led me to the State Library. He strode with purpose across the hushed carpet to the enquiry desk and Celeste.

'Hi, Charles.' She looked up, eyes sparkling.

'It's Sam.'

'Okay,' she said, tilting her head and now examining me closely with a squint.

'What time do you start work tomorrow?' Sam asked.

'Excuse me?'

'I want to take you up in a hot air balloon.'

With wide, uncomprehending eyes, she continued to look at Sam.

'Her English is possibly not so good,' I whispered to Sam.

I may have said this too loudly, for Celeste said, 'Excuse me?'

'What time do you start work?' asked Sam.

'Um. I start at 1pm tomorrow, but I promised a friend—'

'Excuse me,' said an old lady standing behind Sam and me. 'I'm in a rush and want to know when the next addition of *Yarn Magazine* is coming in, and seeing as this is a personal conversation, I see no hesitation in jumping the queue.'

'I do mind you interrupting,' shouted Sam, turning to the woman. The gentle murmuring in the library stopped, and people turned and looked over at Sam. 'Charles and I are asking this lovely woman out, and as soon as she gives us her mobile number, I'll leave you to your enquiry. Now wait your turn.'

'You better give Sam your mobile,' I whispered to a rosy-cheeked Celeste. 'Sam can make a terrible scene, and I don't know what he'll do.'

Celeste took a scrap of paper and scribbled her number.

I took it, and then Sam, winking, said, '*Au revoir*, Celeste.'

Together, Sam and I, with many eyes following us, walked out of the library to a day with the rain gone, the clouds parted, and the sun shining.

CHAPTER 15

THE DIBBLE AND BAINS' BOOK BUYER

'You see what I can do for you, Charles. How many weeks had you been looking at her, too terrified to ask her out? In one go, I got her mobile number. I told you how magnetic and charming I can be,' said Sam, reclining on my couch later that night.

'Yes, thank you. I do appreciate what you did.'

'As for your employees, I put them in their place.'

'I thought you were a bit mean,' I said.

'You're too sweet and trusting for your own good, Charles,' said Sam.

'Look, Sam,' I said, lounging on the same couch and frowning, 'I don't mind what you do to Yamparti, she's cunning, ambitious, and ruthless: the model of a modern left-wing general, and Boris, well he is big and ugly enough to look after himself, but Karen ... I will not have you playing with her. She's been through a great deal with her husband and family.'

'Charles, you're so naive. You heard her husband at the launch. She lied to you about Barry not working. You can't trust a woman like that. She'll be nice to your face one moment, the next, she'll be carving you up in one of her stories. Have you read these?' Sam jumped to his feet and reached for the

ground near the desk where Karen's manuscripts lay. He picked one up and angrily waved it in the mirror.

'*It was Phillip Roth who said that whenever a writer is born, a family dies,*' said Sam. '*And if he knew Karen Tiven, he may have added that the family members are tortured and humiliated in the process.*'

I had to nod with Sam. I had read each manuscript, not all the way through, but enough to know that her words had the potential to tear her family apart. Although Karen touted each manuscript as a work of fiction, it was fiction of the thinnest veneer. No fact or idiosyncrasy of those closest to her escaped dissection and publication. No secret was safe from Karen's pen. From *Estrangement*, I learnt about her daughter's many boyfriends, her painful periods, her battle with weight and self-esteem. From *Addiction*, I learnt about her son's fight with drugs. His rages and fights with his father. The way Karen suspected homosexuality and caught him masturbating at aged fourteen, with a body builder's magazine in hand.

From *Illness*, I learnt all about Barry. How he hated his job as a plumber. How he snored and had problems in the bedroom. Her illicit shipboard romance was visible for all to see in *Under a Samoan Sky*. Her lover, Kane, a creative writing teacher at the University of Arkansas, became Kelvin, a creative writing teacher at the University of Arizona. Her husband back home became Bob, and instead of battling prostate cancer, he fought lung cancer.

Although Karen wrote about those closest to her, she was in fact writing about the most important person in the world: Karen Tiven. At the heart of each manuscript, a brave victim just like Karen (Kay in *Estrangement*, Kassie in *Addiction*, Katie in *Under a Samoan Sky*, and Kathy in *Illness*), writing in the first person, records her emotional struggles against the odds. The unfair demands placed upon her by society, by those closest to her, especially men. How selfish they were, in not recognising the pain their actions caused her. How she was a delicate flower, waiting for the right person to nurture her into fruition.

'Her writing, Charlie boy, is longwinded, cliché ridden, maudlin and lachrymose rubbish. It is victimology without any self-awareness,' said Sam. *'As well as having the potential to destroy many lives. It needs to be repressed.'*

'I don't agree with you Sam,' I said.

'She should be punished like all other writers,' Sam replied, slapping the couch.

'No, Sam, you have her all wrong,' I said. 'She doesn't realise that what she is doing is wrong. She's just another of society's victims. What she really needs is our help,' I said, pouring another glass of Penfolds shiraz for Sam and myself. 'She needs to be nurtured. Helped.'

Sam, clearly tired from the day's exploits, yawned. *'You know you're right, Charlie boy, we should do something for her. Lift her spirits,'* he said, putting down his glass. *'I suddenly feel sorry for the way I treated her today. Let's do something nice for her.'*

I caught Sam's mischievous smile in the mirror.

I was learning to expect the unexpected with Sam. Sam, of course, found the twenty sheets of Dibble and Bains' letterhead in my top draw. Nan worked there for a time as a bookkeeper in the nineties. She used to say they would have published Mum if she had lived long enough. Somehow, I found their letterhead in one of Nan's draws and kept it as a memento, another talisman of my mother's memory. I realised now I was meant to have it and give it to Sam.

Sam wrote it out longhand before I typed it up, then after several drafts, and testing the right way to position the letterhead in the printer, Sam pressed 'print', and this was what came out:

Karen Tiven

Flat 76 Minorca Building

258/260 Flinders Lane

Melbourne 3000

Dear Ms Tiven,

Your four unpublished manuscripts: *Estrangement*, *Addiction*, *Illness* and *Under a Samoan Sky* have come to our attention through Charles Western. After reading all these works, we would like to offer you a book deal to publish all four. We will contact you shortly to discuss contractual arrangements. Our starting offer is $150,000 for each novel. Please be prepared to accept our call anytime from the offices of *Imagine*, Flinders Lane.

We also request you keep this letter a secret, and do not endeavour to call us. 'Operation Tiven' is top secret, and not all the people in the office are aware of or will approve of this offer. A wrong word, even innocently said, may jeopardise the entire project.

Yours sincerely,

J. Alfred Prufrock

Senior Book Buyer

'But won't she recognise the name?' I asked.

'Remember, Charlie boy, she's a writer not a reader.'

'But don't you think the letter is a little bit amateurish?' I asked. 'She'll see straight through it.'

Sam laughed. *'Karen is a gullible fool desperate to be published. Nigerian Princes and scammers in Indian call centres prey on people like Karen every day. She'll fall for it. Just you wait and see.'*

CHAPTER 16

AN EXPENSIVE RESTAURANT

Karen, Yamparti and Boris didn't return to the office the next day.
'We've lost our staff,' I said.

Sam could only chuckle. *'They'll be back. They know they're on a good wicket. Besides, who else would employ these people and publish their stories.'*

Sure enough, they returned on Wednesday.

Yamparti arriving first — sheepishly, I thought, when she sat behind her computer, not daring to look up, as if afraid of whom she might find: Charles or Sam. She didn't speak for most of the morning. In fact, she kept quiet even when Boris burst through the door.

'Why did you tell the police you didn't know me?' cried Boris.

Sam spoke up. 'Because, although Charles might know you, I haven't been fully introduced.'

'You're mad, Charles, mad. I spent all night in the police lock-up with drug addicts, thieves, and scum.'

'As a writer, you should have felt right at home,' said Sam.

Boris reddened, both his palms curling into fists. He looked as if he wanted to hit Sam. I thought it best to intervene.

'I know it's a terrible experience, Boris, but consider it as good material for your novels; one day you'll look back at the incident and be thankful.'

'Thankful!' cried Boris. 'Being locked up with drug addicts, my friends lying to the police.'

'Let me make it up to you,' I said, rising to my feet as Karen made her way into the office. 'I'll take you all out to lunch at a fancy restaurant.'

'What now?' said Boris, consulting his watch. 'It's ten am.'

'You're working for a magazine now. Long liquid lunches, beginning early and ending late into the night are the norm now.'

Sam and I led the three others to the European restaurant in Spring Street. Nan had taken me here once for her birthday, and I found the food both tasty and expensive. I ordered the salt-roasted châteaubriand for two, with fat chips, béarnaise sauce, blue cheese, and endive salad. I persuaded Karen to try the king fillet, while Boris tucked into the Greek lamb. Meanwhile, Yamparti ditched her vegetarianism and socialism to choose the selected caviars.

After completing the main course and coffee, Sam ordered the champagne. He ordered two bottles of Gosset Grande Millésime, then pouring out a glass for the others, he proposed a toast to the magazine. After a sip, Sam chinked his glass for silence, then rising to his feet, he made the following impromptu speech.

'Thank you for all coming to lunch. As you know, this is my first working week at the magazine, but I believe I'm safe in saying Charles has created something special. It's not easy plucking something from the imagination and making it cold hard reality. If Charles has one genius, it is the genius of turning fantasy into reality. I'm so happy to have this opportunity to lead you towards his creative vision.'

It must have been the expensive French champagne, for the others smiled and nodded approvingly. Sam would fix that.

'It's therefore with great pleasure,' continued Sam, 'that I announce a new direction for the magazine. As of the next issue, we'll only publish fiction. No more politics, no more criticism, no more articles bemoaning the fate of some flea-bitten race or group no one gives a stuff about. I believe the following adage is correct: go woke, go broke.'

Yamparti's eyes widened.

'As well as this, we'll be selective in our choice of fiction. No more feminist fiction, no more maudlin confessions of middle-aged women, no more plot boilers or airport thrillers from Serbian immigrants. Instead, we'll only publish absurdist fiction.' Sam stopped there and sculled his champagne before pouring another glass.

The others looked at each other, clearly not certain what to say or even what to think. Boris especially looked like he wanted to lash out at the Serbian crack but was unsure whether he heard correctly or not. Only Karen continued to smile, as if Sam's speech had sailed well and truly over her head.

Finally, Yamparti broke the awkward silence. 'What is absurdist literature?'

'Absurdist fiction is one that begins with an outrageous proposition,' said Sam. 'Let us say: writers are vain, greedy and self-absorbed creatures. Hold on, I can't use that as an example, as it's a self-evident truth. Instead, let us say a story beginning with the absurd proposition that: libraries are cruel and terrible places. The writer then spends the rest of the story, not only proving it, but making the story so real that the reader comes to believe that the absurd is possible, and the possible is even more absurd than he or she ever imagined.'

I listened to Sam's words, marvelling at their eccentric coherence. I wondered where he would take it next.

Sam snapped his fingers. He requested a pen and paper from the waiter. Then turning to the table, he said, 'As loyal employees of *Imagine*, it's your responsibility to take this concept and flesh it out into a manifesto.'

'Excuse me?' asked Yamparti. 'You want us to do what?'

'I want you to revolutionise twenty-first century literature,' cried Sam. 'Anything less is unacceptable. Now, if you'll excuse me, I need to step outside for a moment.' Sam sculled his champagne, then grabbing the unopened bottle of Gosset Grande Millésime, he walked outside into the bright sunshine.

I followed him to the top of Collins Street, and then we kept on walking down the hill back to the office. 'Shouldn't we go back and pay?' I asked.

'Why should we? Let them pay for a change. It'll do them the world of good. Besides, it's another experience they can use in their stories.'

We returned to the office, the mail waiting for us, which included Karen's letter. Sam placed it prominently on her workstation; then we eased into our seat, placing our feet on the desk, popping the unopened bottle of champagne, foamy liquid running down our arm before we sculled. As expected, the phone rang.

Sam answered it with a foreign accent. 'Olla!'

'Charles, thank god it's you. It's Yamparti. We have a problem with the bill.'

'No comprende. Me speak no ENGLISH.'

'Charles, stop this! I know it's you.'

'Senorita, me no speak Anglaise. Wait till boss come back. One hour.' Sam hung up.

It rang furiously a few more times. I wanted so much to answer it, dear reader. Truly I did. I felt so terrible about leaving them there, but Sam wouldn't hear of me returning to pay. Finally, the phone stopped ringing.

Around 3.30pm, the three amigos ambled into the office. Controlled fury was the way Sam later described their collective expressions.

'You left us high and dry,' said Yamparti.

'The lunch cost over six hundred dollars,' said Boris.

'I don't have that type of money. I have a family to raise, an invalid husband,' added Karen.

'We need to speak to you, Charles,' said Yamparti grabbing her chair and sliding it up to my desk.

Boris grabbed his chair also and positioned it next to Yamparti's.

'We don't know what is happening in your life at the moment, and we don't want to pry, but all of us are extremely worried about your behaviour.'

'Oh!'

'Dropping our pay out the window, leaving us to pay the bill at the restaurant, the sudden changes in direction for the magazine,' said Boris.

'And then there is the small matter of "Sam",' said Yamparti.

'We have nothing against Sam,' added Boris.

'Of course,' said Yamparti, retaking charge of the conversation, 'he has his charms. However, we believe what you need right now are loyal friends. Friends who will help you run your magazine. I think I speak for the three of us.' She looked at Boris, then Karen, who didn't acknowledge Yamparti's glance. Karen stood in the middle of the room, her eyes agog, her mouth open as she read from a letter.

Yamparti continued, 'If you need to take time off for whatever reason ... deal with whatever issues may be in your life ... I want you to know, Charles, we'll be here for you. We'll keep your dream alive. Won't we.' Yamparti turned to Boris, who nodded and added, 'Of course.' Yamparti's eyes then fell next on Karen, who was still standing in the middle of the room, staring open-mouthed at her letter. 'Karen!' shouted Yamparti.

Karen jumped, the letter trembling in her hands before she clasped it tightly in her fingers and hastily folded it into her pocket. She looked as if she had woken from an ecstatic dream.

'I was just explaining to Charles what we discussed at lunch,' continued Yamparti.

'At lunch?' repeated Karen, dreamily.

'Yes,' said Yamparti through clenched teeth. 'How we were really worried about Charles.'

'Charles, of course, sweet caring Charles,' said Karen, coming over to my desk. 'If you need anything, Charles, anything at all, consider it done. If you have any worries, then I'm here for you.'

They wanted to marginalise Sam ...

Sam rose to his feet and walked to the window. 'So, you want to know what worries Charles?' he said, pulling up the blind. 'Why he has been acting so strangely?'

'Yes, we do,' said Yamparti.

'Then come over here and behold the view.'

The three walked over to Sam.

Sam threw his arms over Boris' shoulder. 'Look down at the street below and tell me what you see.'

Boris looked hesitantly at Sam and I, before looking out the window. 'Um, I see the road and a rubbish bin—'

'No!' cried Sam.

Boris trembled.

'Down there are four million stories waiting to be told. Think of all those hopes, dreams and loves all walking below our feet with nobody there to capture them. That's what's making Charles very, very angry! We are up here and not down there recording it. BORIS! YAMPARTI!' Sam snapped his fingers. 'Get a pen and notebook. I want you on the street, right this minute. I want you to stop people and ask them for their life story, and I want you to write it down and keep writing until they stop.'

'You want us to do what?' said Boris.

'I want you recording the hopes and dreams of this city,' said Sam. 'Before they are lost forever.'

'I thought you wanted only fiction in your magazine,' said Yamparti.

'I've changed my mind,' said Sam. 'From now on, we're going to be the mirror of this city.'

Boris and Yamparti stared at Sam incredulously.

'This is a wonderful idea. Isn't it, Karen?' said Sam.

'It *is* wonderful,' she repeated, like one under hypnosis.

'Don't you think, Boris and Yamparti would profit greatly from listening to the people?' said Sam, addressing Karen.

'Of course.'

'Well, you heard Karen. Get down on the street,' said Sam. 'This magazine offers you the chance of self-improvement, and you stand there with your mouths open like Luna Park clowns. Get down on the street. NOW!' Sam shooed them to the door, as one would a pigeon who had inadvertently flown inside from an open window.

Boris and Yamparti, with a mixture of surprise and fear at Sam's unpredictable and loud manner, took their pens and notebooks and left the office.

'Remember also to take a photo of them with your mobile phone for the next edition,' Sam shouted before slamming shut the door.

'You have so many wonderful ideas,' said Karen.

'I know,' said Sam. 'I know.'

Sam offered Karen the rest of the day off, but she wanted to stay, so Sam gave her my notes from the State Library to type. This was convenient, and I busied myself with a list of office and personal chores for Karen to do.

Around five pm, the phone rang.

Even though it was on my desk, Karen leapt on it. 'Karen Tiven speaking,' she said, sounding like a love-struck schoolgirl hoping Prince Charming was on the other end of the line. Sadly, the excitement in her voice waned as she passed it over to me.

'It's your nan.'

'Hello, Nan,' I said, taking the phone. 'Why didn't you call my mobile?'

'It always goes to voice mail. Now, Charles, I'm cooking you a steak with pepper sauce. I thought you might like to come over.'

'Who else have you invited?'

This was one of Nan's favourite ruses. She would invite me to dinner with the promise of one of my favourite dishes. I would accept and go to dinner under the impression it would just be Nan and me, only to discover Nan had invited a young girl, usually a granddaughter of one of her friends. After serving dinner, Nan would be overcome with a headache that required her immediate withdrawal from the dinner, and I would be left to entertain the young lady, with special instructions to show her mum's wedding photos.

'Are you trying your hand at matchmaking again?'

'Really, Charles, you have my intentions all wrong.'

'Who have you invited?'

She sighed. 'I thought I would have Mr Smith, my accountant, over for dinner. I've been telling him all about your magazine. I know you don't want me interfering, but Mr Smith is always good for business advice.'

'I'm not interested,' I said.

But from the corner of my mind, Sam whispered, *'Go! Go!'*

I didn't want to listen to the wisdom of a business accountant, but something about Sam's eager manner told me that he did.

Mr Smith

Mr Smith was certainly different from how I imagined him to be. Instead of a middle-aged, severe, and humourless 'suit', I met Terry, in his early thirties, a warm handshake, a big smile, with a happy hail, good-fellow manner. He certainly had a hearty appetite, eating three servings of apple pie. While he stuffed his mouth with food, he talked happily with Nan about his three passions: his family, sailing, and the Hawthorn Football Club. It was only after his second cup of real coffee, and Nan having retired for the night, that he pushed away his plate, reclined in his seat and burped out, 'So, your nan says you've started a magazine.'

'That's right,' I said, taking the lead. 'A literary one.'

'Tricky business, publishing,' said Terry. 'I know a few people in the game. Frankly, there isn't much money to be made, unless that is … you sell a magazine people really want to read. Unfortunately, Australia has such a small population, it's difficult to make a go of specialist magazines, especially literary ones. Not many people these days want to read magazines dedicated to fiction. I don't want to be presumptuous,' said Terry, pushing back his seat and stretching his legs.

'Be as presumptuous as you want,' said Sam, butting in. 'We like presumptuous people.'

A flitter of incomprehension clouded Terry's face before his brain filed it as a joke, no doubt, and a smile creased his sated face. 'What's your target audience?'

'University students, predominately.'

'Have you looked at what advertising other magazines catering for university students run?'

'Um … not really,' I admitted.

'Do you know what your weekly outgoings are?'

'No.'

'Do you have a business plan?

'Pardon?'

'The business plan is your road map to achieving it. Unless a business has one, it's hard to succeed. You see, to make a success of any venture, you must put your efforts and resources into things that will achieve your objectives. I see too many businesses in my practice spending too much of their resources on things that don't forward their business. Do you know what you want to do with the magazine?'

I didn't know what to say. I reddened at my stupidity and Terry's expectant gaze. I had set up a magazine, and like a fool, I failed to grasp the first rule of business. Asking, what I wanted to achieve? My father would have been ashamed of my stupidity. Luckily, Sam, who had been champing at the bit all dinner to speak, jumped in to cover my embarrassment.

'So, you want to know why Charles is in business? What his dream is? What makes him get up in the morning? What makes him tick?'

Terry knitted his eyebrows and nodded.

'Charles had a dream,' continued Sam, 'to brighten up this dreary world through imaginative, creative and inspiring writing.' Sam stopped here and took a sip of wine before continuing, 'Writing, to Charles, was a mystical, mysterious process, more magical than mechanical, more alchemy than an arduous slog in front of a computer screen. And the writers who wrote were in part divine beings with the deepest understanding of life itself. It was as if by locking themselves away from the world and writing, they weren't only giving life to stories, but tapping into the deepest, richest and most profound well of existence. And if they were sometimes less than perfect — vain, selfish, and treacherous — then that was the price we all paid for the truths they told, the treasures they unearthed, and the beauty they showed. Charles wanted so much to be a part of that world. To help and nurture many writers. But then Charles started his magazine and saw writers up close and personal. He met egotistical, selfish and treacherous people, who he mistakenly believed were capable of great writing. How disappointed he was when he read their words. Worthless. Terrible. Charles realised, to his horror, that writers were incapable of good behaviour, that the act of writing was a form of madness; a practice akin to smoking crack cocaine, which reduced the practitioners to creatures no better than self-absorbed zombies, hurting and destroying all those around them. Writers weren't people to be admired, but feared, and where possible … stopped. That's Charles' great goal, to stop the mounds of awful writing thrown into the cultural landscape. Where possible, to crush a writer's spirit, shake them from their madness. Make them realise the pain and suffering they cause others. How they aren't holier than thou, or they have some divine right to treat people the way they do, or that they have some special knowledge, because they happened to put one word after another. There are too many people writing in this world. Charles' job is to stop them. That is his life's goal.' Sam stopped there, sculling the rest of the wine in one gulp. I only realised then that he had been trembling as he spoke. I was shocked by what he said. Did he really mean it? Was it true? Was Sam this unhinged?

'I see,' said Terry, wide-eyed and unblinking, as if seeing Sam for the first time that evening and being unsure whether he disapproved or thought him mad.

'Is that what you believe, Charles?'

I said nothing as Sam lowered his voice and propped himself across the table. 'It's not so much a suspicion, but a feeling, that one of Charles' employees is stealing from the magazine. I know it's a terrible and slanderous thing to say, and I have no proof, but I thought … with a man like you in charge of the books, you could keep an eye not only on Boris, but all the people at *Imagine*.'

Silence followed.

I blushed at Sam's temerity. His bald-faced lie.

A watchful Terry Smith finally said, 'I can't do it. But I do know some fraud investigators who can help.'

Sam took from my coat pocket my chequebook.

Terry's eyes fell upon it, a note of disapproval creasing his brow.

'What's your price?' asked Sam.

'I don't have one,' said Terry, the humorous and jolly manner now replaced by a stern and serious accountant.

'Everyone has a price.'

'I don't want your money.'

'But I will offer you three times what you make in a week.'

Terry sighed and leant forward again, this time with a deep frown. 'I'm not taking your money, Charles. I wouldn't feel right about it.'

'Why not? It's only money,' said Sam. 'Everyone wants it. Everyone needs it.'

Terry sighed again, and then he considered me carefully, like a doctor might study a new and disagreeable symptom of a favourite patient. 'I hope I'm not out of line by what I say next,' he said.

'Be out of line as much as you like,' said Sam. 'Charles and I like it when people speak out of line.'

'I don't believe you're interested at all in making money. Furthermore, I don't believe you're all that interested in writing or literature. You have some personal issues with the people you work with. Maybe this employee you spoke about has stolen from you, maybe not. But one thing is certain, you want to toy with these people. Maybe writers are vain and treacherous people, as you say, capable of inflicting pain on others, but Charles, I hear you're also a writer. From what your nan tells me, a good one at that. You seem intent on doing to your employees what you claim writers do to others. I might only be a boring accountant, not much respected or valued by creative intellectual types like you, but I love my job. I believe that with my talent for figures I can help people fulfil their dreams. That's what most small businesspeople are, people like yourself with a dream, a vision. I just help them reach their potential. However, I doubt whether you're interested in my skills. You just want to use me in one of your games. What you need, Charles, is a psychologist.' Terry stopped there and again studied me closely, as if trying to gauge the effect of his words, if any.

Sam had so much to say. I could feel him yearning to speak. I hushed him. 'I thank you for your honesty,' I said to Terry. 'Do you have a business card? When I'm ready, I'll give you a call.'

'Of course.' Terry smiled. He reached into his pocket and took out his business card and offered it to me. Terry then lifted his glass of wine.

I refilled my glass and raised it too.

'To the future,' said Terry.

We clinked on that, then Terry selected another piece of apple pie and ate. I watched him eat it, all the while thinking, thinking ...

'What you said tonight was out of line,' I muttered to Sam as we returned home by Uber.

'Excuse me?' said the Uber driver, waking from his own daydream.

I ignored him.

'What did I say that was so wrong?' Sam asked.

'You came across as arrogant and pompous, not to mention, you accused Boris of stealing.' I noted the frown of the Uber driver, his raised eyebrow in the rear-vision mirror.

'All I was doing was covering your embarrassment for not doing your homework on the magazine. Launching it without proper analysis.'

'I told you, I follow my heart.'

'And look where it got you,' he said. *'Yamparti, Karen and Boris.'*

'You accused Boris of stealing.'

'All I was doing was having a little fun.'

'Well, I don't like it. From now on you say nothing and only speak when I need you.'

'You're really boring, Charles Western.'

'So what, I like boring.'

'You might like boring, but does Celeste?'

Sam was certainly daring and bold. Willing to do things I would shrink from. But tonight, he crossed a line. Sure, Boris was an annoying racist, but to imply he stole? As for the letter to Karen …

While I drifted to sleep that night, a new and troubling thought entered my consciousness. What if I couldn't control Sam?

I opened the top drawer of my bedside table and took the bottle of pills. I rattled them before putting them back in the drawer and closing it with a slam. I could control Sam. I could control Sam, I repeated as I drifted off to sleep.

CHAPTER 18

BALLOON RIDE

With my arms metaphorically thrown over my head like a suffocating blanket, I fell subconsciously onto my knees, crouching as low as possible in the basket as we left the ground and made our ascent into the sky.

Why did Sam have to invite her for a hot air balloon ride on our first date? Didn't he know how scared, I, Charles Western, was of heights? Especially after my father plunged three hundred metres to his death.

'You're such a nervous nelly, Charlie boy. Are you forever going to be bound by your phobias? By past failures? By Brains? By Raven?' asked Sam that morning as we dressed.

'Why not go rollerblading, or ice skating, or dancing? Why start off with ballooning?' I said, addressing the mirror.

'Because she is going out with me and not fearful and timid Charles.' Sam laughed.

The tingling began at my penis and rose all the way to the base of my skull as the basket left the earth.

'It's magnificent,' said Celeste.

'Melbourne is very flat,' said Sam, shaking his head.

'Look! You can see a tanker on the bay going through the heads. It looks no bigger than my hand,' she said, pushing away her hair blown by the wind into her face. 'Oh my, look at the traffic down there. Everything looks so small up here.'

What was I doing, cowering down here? I should be the one standing next to Celeste, not Sam. I couldn't live in fear for the rest of my life. I rose to my feet and took Sam's place by Celeste, keeping my eyes riveted the whole time to her face, enjoying the view vicariously through the emotions of wonder, awe and happiness reflected in her eyes. Occasionally, she turned to smile at me and point towards some object, but I kept my eyes firmly locked on her face, anything than looking down.

'Why are you staring?' she finally asked.

'Because you're so beautiful, Celeste,' I said. 'Also, I'm terrified if I look down, I might faint.'

Celeste laughed. She laughed so long and hard, the others in the basket stopped and stared.

'If you're afraid of heights, Charles, why did you invite me up in a hot air balloon?' she asked finally. Thankfully, the balloon was descending when she said this.

'I didn't invite you, Sam did. He thought you would be impressed by this. He's a different person from me.'

Celeste tilted her head and squinted. 'You're an unusual person, Charles. So different from any of the men I've gone out with before.'

'I hope in a good way?'

Eventually and thankfully, the basket kissed the ground again. Taking her hand, I helped her out of the basket. She didn't take back her hand straightaway but let it linger in mine the few metres it took us to reach the footpath.

'Why did you get Sam to ask me out?' she queried as we boarded the 109 tram to the city.

'Because … Because I was afraid of you. Terrified of your beauty, really,' I admitted. 'I've been meaning to ask you out for weeks, but terror and indecision held me back. I didn't know what I would do if you said no, so I got Sam to do it.'

'Oh, that is so sweet,' she said, touching her heart.

'Sam is different from me in so many ways,' I said. 'He doesn't give a damn what other people think. He plunges in where others fear to tread. I don't think I could have asked you out without him.'

'I am fascinated by your use of Sam. I'm studying psychology and want to know more. Why Sam?' she enquired as we sat down for breakfast at a café near Flinders Street Station

From our window seat, I considered the pedestrians spilling across the street, and the clocks over the entrance to the station.

'All my life, I've lived in the shadows of other people,' I finally said, turning to face Celeste. 'There was my father. He was a successful businessman. I was always in awe of his tenacity and ability to create a multi-million-dollar business from the ground up. He would holler and bark at people, but they loved him for it. Yet when I tried to emulate him, it came out all wrong. Then there's my nan. She raised me single-handedly and is a force to be reckoned with. She was always telling me what to do and how to act, though she always did it in a kind way, always with my best interest at heart. I never really had the heart to stand up to her. Then there were the bullies at school. I never had any way of countering their taunts and mockery. Now with my magazine, I need to direct people. Tell them what to do. In a weak moment, I found Sam. He's my way of being that larger-than-life character, like my father, without losing my own personality. Sam does the hard, difficult jobs, while allowing me the space to be the best version of myself.'

I stared out the window again.

Celeste said nothing, clearly waiting for me to speak, sensing correctly that I had more to say, and leaving me the space to formulate the rest of my answer.

'Then there was my mother,' I said, turning to gaze at Celeste. 'I've lived in the shadow of her all my life.' I stopped there and stared out the window again. The morning, which had started out so sunny, was now drab with rain. Without expecting it or wanting it, tears fell from my eyes. 'She died giving birth to me, and I feel such guilt for her death. Every single day it hangs over me. I feel as if I should be honouring her memory with some great deed. But then I think that maybe I'm not worthy of the sacrifice.' I stopped there, and taking a deep breath, I wiped my eyes with a spare napkin. My face burnt. What an idiot I was. I had embarrassed myself. How she must think I'm weak, soppy, a little boy instead of a man. I gazed at my uneaten bacon and eggs, not wanting to look at Celeste's face. Yet her hand touched mine.

'I'm so sorry, Charles,' she said, tears falling down her own face. 'I know what it is like to lose a mother so soon.' She squeezed my hand gently.

'Oh,' I said. 'How?'

'My mother passed away from cancer when I was two. My sister and I were raised by my maternal grandmother. My father, as a navy officer, spent long stretches away from home and couldn't spend it looking after children.'

'Oh, Celeste, you *do* know what it's like,' I said. 'Is that why you left France. To escape from the pain? To run from the sadness?'

'No, not at all. I've come to terms with my mother's death. I came to Australia to experience another country and culture, that's all.'

'Sometimes, I wish I could go and live in Russia or Mongolia, far from my nan and everyone I know. I feel so much pressure sometimes, to live up to the sacrifice of my mother. I don't think I'll ever get over her death.'

'You will. It will come,' she said, taking my hand and squeezing it again.

This time, I didn't let it go but held it gently in mine. 'You're so kind,' I said, wiping the tears from my eyes. 'So, you're studying psychology.' I wanted to change the subject as quickly as possible. 'You're in luck. I have enough neuroses for a whole semester of study!'

'That's why I'm fascinated with you and Sam,' she said with a laugh.

'I'm glad someone is fascinated by me,' I replied, grinning.

'So, how do you decide whether it will be you or Sam?' she asked. 'Is there any potion that you drink?'

'Oh no. It depends on the situation really. One minute it's Charles Western, and the next, Sam's in charge. It just happens,' I said. 'I hope you don't think me crazy?'

'Of course not. I think it's fascinating.'

'He is my Dr Jekyll to my Mr Hyde,' I added.

'You'll find it the other way around,' said Celeste. 'Dr Jekyll was the doctor and the sane one, and Mr Hyde was crazy.'

'Dr Jekyll sounds a crazier name, don't you think? Mr Hyde sounds so normal.'

'I've never thought of it like that,' she revealed.

After breakfast, we walked up Swanston Street towards the Queen Victoria Market, speaking about the small, incidental things in life. Along the way, I bought Celeste a single red rose from a street flower seller. She blushed the same colour and smelt it a long time while I examined her face closely.

Finally, and too soon, we reached Celeste's accommodation. She boarded with a distant cousin in a small terrace house in North Melbourne.

'I've really enjoyed my morning with you, Celeste. I'd like to take you out to dinner.'

'You or Sam?'

'I'm asking you out,' I said. 'No Mr Hyde.'

'I'd love to,' she replied, smelling her rose.

'Well, I need to get to work,' I said, putting out my hand for a handshake.

'You idiot,' Sam whispered, and he leant forward with his lips.

Celeste turned her head, and we were left to kiss her cheek before she disappeared inside.

CHAPTER 19

Sam's Revenge

I headed back to the office whistling, amazed at how well it had gone. Sam had behaved, falling into the background when asked. I could really handle him.

I had only stepped into Centre Place Laneway when a familiar voice out of the cacophony of sounds and smells arrested my step. I hunted for it among the moving bodies.

Yamparti, on the corner of Flinders Lane and Centre Place, with her head bent, paced to-and-fro, talking on her mobile. 'It was good to meet you at the launch, Eugene ... And thank you for the opportunity to edit Ki Goonawanda's novel. This is such a great honour. Please thank him for me,' she said.

Sam and I stepped back against the wall and blended into the scenery. Our ears pitched to attention over the echoing footsteps of pedestrians to Yamparti's voice.

'I know you said you're a lawyer and you also know Charles. I was wondering if you can help me ... Charles has gone completely crazy. I think he's insane. I know he owns the magazine, but can you find some law related to insanity that I can use to lessen his influence? I don't care if he owns it. It's not fair he should tell me how to run it. You must find some law, any law, which I can use against him. He must be stopped. He has me in the street dictating people's stories, then he rips up what I write, in my face. It's so humiliating. He's turning the magazine into a laughingstock … If it wasn't for him, this magazine would be perfect … You will help me … I appreciate it, Eugene. I'll look over Ki's novel tonight, then send the changes back to you before I send them to Sally. Okay, thanks, much appreciated, bye.'

Sam motioned for me to follow him. We crept passed Yamparti and into the Minorca building, a twinkle in Sam's eye.

That night after a few drinks, Sam and I turned to the question of Yamparti.

'*You must crush her before she crushes you,*' said Sam.

'Poor Yamparti.' I sighed.

'*How can you say poor Yamparti?*' said Sam, leaping to his feet. '*She's trying to steal your magazine.*'

'She's fighting the good fight, Sam,' I said, wagging my finger into the mirror.

'*Rubbish.*' Sam cackled, collapsing onto the sofa. '*Left-wing intellectuals are all the same. They talk of inclusion and tolerance but really want to do the opposite. Give them half a chance, and they'll steal your property and throw you in jail for looking at them the wrong way.*'

'I feel terribly sorry for both her and Eugene,' I admitted.

'*Eugene, really?*' Sam snorted. *Why?*

'Because he's fighting against overwhelming forces, Sam. He's fighting the forces of conservatism, Christianity, and the patriarchy. He and Yamparti are lone voices crying in the wilderness. The forces of reaction ready to crush them at any time.'

Sam stretched out on the couch as I pressed home my point.

'We can't let Eugene publish his manuscript in its present form. Attacking the Catholic Church? That'll only end in his ruin; and ridiculing the conservative political parties ... that will end his career. See it now, Sam, a group of young conservatives, forsaking a cheese and wine night at the Camberwell Town Hall to turn up unannounced at the offices of *Imagine*, dragging Yamparti kicking and screaming away, using their powers and influence to cancel Eugene, and destroy any future career they might have.'

Sam must have seen these visions too and leapt to his feet. '*Yes, you're right, we have to save them,*' he cried. '*We have to save them before it's too late.*' Sam turned on the laptop and found the electronic version of Ki Goonawanda's novel he had surreptitiously copied onto my USB stick from Yamparti's computer.

'*I'm so glad we live in the twenty-first century,*' said Sam. '*How much easier it would have been for Tolstoy to write* War and Peace *with a laptop and Microsoft Word. I'm sure Tolstoy secretly hated the name Pierre Bezukhov by the time he finished writing his novel. But after fifteen books and two epilogues, there was no way he'd even attempt changing the name of his protagonist from Pierre to Darryl, even for a dogged writer like Tolstoy.*'

'Tolstoy would have got his wife Sophia to do the changes,' I added as way of clarification.

'*But don't forget, Charles, as well as being Tolstoy's amanuensis, she raised thirteen children. I'm sure even she would have baulked at the mammoth task of making this change,*' said Sam.

Ah, the glories of Microsoft Office. With one keyboard stroke, Sam could change the word 'Christianity' to 'Islam,' and 'church' to 'mosque.' With a few more strokes of the keyboard, 'God' became 'Allah,' and the 'Bible' became the 'Koran', and of course, 'Jesus freaks' became 'Mohamed freaks'.

Then Sam struck difficulty with hazy terms such as 'conservative' and 'neoliberal'. 'Labor' and 'socialists' were extensively auditioned, until Sam settled with: 'leftist types'. He reasoned that these *leftist types* would be far more forgiving of a good prodding from an up-and-coming writer, than those nasty conservatives: more likely to turn the other cheek and forgive and forget; especially when handing out grant money.

As for the extensive references to Indigenous names and settings, these were changed to Anglo-Saxon, Celtic and Scottish ones.

Sam printed out the changes, and we read it afresh.

The story was now quite good, in a surreal way. It was set in the near future. A Labor prime minister, Mohammed Abdalla — a lying Mohamed freak, with a penchant for cross-dressing and the scuttling of boats carrying Jewish asylum seekers — now controlled Canberra, after calling martial law and outlawing all dissent. But a few brave souls still cared, still took the fight to the Labor types. The hero of the piece, Dustan (formerly Daku, in the original), a young Scottish university drop-out, and intellectual, fond of quoting English dreamtime poets such as Dylan Thomas and playing his bazooka, meets the gorgeous Fatima, a lap-dancing refugee from a strict Muslim family. Unwittingly, they become Australia's most wanted after destroying Mohamed's Mosque in the heart of Melbourne. Somehow their wild lovemaking on the mosque altar (there were a few minor details in the book that didn't ring true) knocked over a candle that set fire to the altar cloth, which helped burn down the mosque. They also became unwitting leaders of the Hayek freedom fighters, (Sam extensively auditioned Adam Smith revolutionaries, even Ludwig Von Mises terrorists, before settling on good old Hayek). Together, Fatima and Dustan go on the run, meeting a wide variety of eccentric characters.

The manuscript was littered with quotes from an assortment of obscure Indigenous intellectuals, Dreamtime stories, references to the cultural paucity of Australian suburbia, the stifling effect of Islam, the rampant consumption and blatant racism within Indigenous communities. Finally, this odd and angry novel concluded with Fatima stabbing Prime Minister Mohammed Abdalla, before shooting herself. An act intended to set Australia and Dustan free.

After reading it through, Sam thought it lacked something.

I struggled to see how it could be improved.

'It needs a scholarly introduction from Yamparti extolling its virtues, Charlie boy,' suggested Sam. *'And for this to be put into the magazine. You know she's put the first chapter in the next edition.'*

With a few glasses of Barossa Valley Shiraz, for inspiration, Sam completed the one- thousand-word essay.

In it, Yamparti waxed lyrically on the manuscript from Ki Goonawanda, who she revealed as the pen name of one Eugene Whiteford, an old Victoria Grammarian. She loved the way Ki (Eugene), in *Dreamtime in Suburbia*, challenged existing paradigms and exposed the rotten heart of the left. The corrosive effect of radical Islam, as well as the stifling rigidity and intolerance of the Australian progressive class. The essay ended with a lament on the appalling standards of women writers in Australia, and whether women weren't better off not expressing themselves at all, but leaving it to the males, especially those with a private school education, their intellectual betters, to write the story of Australia. The last page of the essay, the one composed on the first glass of the second bottle of red, with its query, as to whether women had gained anything by personal liberation, sounded not only coherent but lyrical.

'But I don't believe women writers are inferior,' I slurred. 'What about Agatha Christie, Daphne Du Maurier, Miles Franklin, Katherine Susannah Prichard.'

'I like them too. I even liked those two Stalinists: Barnard and Eldershaw,' said Sam. *'They wrote that great book,* Tomorrow and Tomorrow. *But this isn't about women writers, Charles. I'm merely having a bit of fun. Besides, I'm sure the feminists will have a big laugh about it. They see the funny side of everything.'* Sam cut and pasted this essay into the first page of the next edition of *Imagine*. *'We should update the entire edition,'* he slurred. *'It needs a thorough edit.'*

'I can't believe I'm self-sabotaging again,' I said. 'This is worse than walking out of my VCE English exam.'

'You're not self-sabotaging, Charles, you're being edgy and daring, livening up a dull magazine. Wait till it hits the universities.' Sam pushed me aside, and cracking his fingers, he said. *'First, let's get rid of Boris' stupid story, Bombing at Midnight.'* With a click of the mouse, Sam sent the story to the trash. *'Now, let's update some of Yamparti's essays also,'* Sam proposed.

'She's possessive of her articles,' I said. 'It might not be a good idea.'

'I don't intend to radically change them or alter their intent. I will merely change one or two words. How could she complain if we change only a few?'

I fretted and didn't want to make these changes, but what could I do? Sam now sat at the laptop, the cursor hovering over the 'find and replace' function.

In the article denouncing toxic masculinity in our society, Sam replaced the word 'masculinity' with 'femininity'. In the article titled 'Injustice in Palestine', Sam changed 'Palestinian' for 'Israeli'. However, with these changes, entire paragraphs needed to be substantially reedited.

'I thought you said you were changing only one or two words?'

'I'm not changing its intent,' said Sam. *'Just making it more coherent.'* Next, Sam altered the essay on transgenderism to note Yamparti's displeasure at the blurring of sex boundaries. 'There are only two sexes,' Yamparti opined, 'male and female, as the good Lord intended, and no amount of surgery can turn a transgender man into a female or vice versa.'

After finishing the changes, Sam and I both rose to our feet and saluted the bravery of both Yamparti and Eugene, before sculling our glass in their honour.

'What do we do now?' I slurred. 'Where do we send it?'

'We send the completed manuscript, with a copy of Yamparti's accompanying essay, to Dibble and Bains.'

'We can't,' I said. 'They'll know it's us.'

'You forget, Charlie boy, there are writers who will do anything to be famous. Absolutely anything.'

CHAPTER 20

MR PRUFROCK'S VERY IMPORTANT QUESTION

The next morning, which was a Saturday, we put a call in to the office on our way to buy coffee. As expected, the phone answered straightaway.

'Karen Tiven speaking.'

'Karen Tiven, this is J. Alfred Prufrock.'

'Mr Prufrock, I'm so glad you called. I've been waiting by the phone, as you said.'

'Good, and continue to do that. Now, listen carefully, I don't have much time, as I'm off to ask a very important question.'

'Is it about my manuscript?' asked Karen, her voice tingling with excitement and expectation.'

'Oh, do not ask what it is, let me first go make my visit.'

'I understand, Mr Prufrock. Anything you say, Mr Prufrock.'

'And now, I have an important task for you to perform.'

'Oh.'

Even over the rumbling of a passing tram, I could make out the excited tremor of her voice.

'Two packages will be delivered to the offices of *Imagine* today,' said J.

Alfred Prufrock, deepening his voice. 'I need you to deliver each package in person to the following two addresses today. The first is the Carlton Mosque, in Drummond Street. Give it to whoever is there and tell them the manuscript is a gift from one Australian writer to their religion. Deliver the second package to the main administration offices of Dibble and Bains, in Brunswick. Ask for Ms Sally Diamond. Tell her it is the completed drafts of the manuscript discussed on the phone. She'll know what it means.'

'Which of my manuscripts are you sending?' purred Karen.

'Oh, do not ask which one it is. First, go and make your visit.'

'Okay. Okay,' she said.

'Your words Mrs Tiven will echo across the globe. Your characters will cry, Mrs Tiven, and a million women will cry with them.'

'Oh, Mr Prufrock, I do thank you. I thank you ever so much.'

'Don't thank me. Instead, thank the human imagination that made this, made me, and all that is to come, possible.'

'You're a wise man,' said Karen. Another tram rumbled past, so Sam and I lost her voice for a time, but when the noise subsided, we found ourselves with a new tone, timid but curious. 'There is a small question of contract. When should we—'

'Only after you perform one other small task.'

'Another?'

'The courier will also deliver an envelope. Inside this will be a USB port, with the changes for the next edition of *Imagine*. This must be sent to the printer with strict instructions they are the final drafts for that edition, and they are to start printing and distributing straightaway. Also, I want you to upload this to the website.'

'But Mr Prufrock, the editor Yamparti is the only one who can approve that.'

'I have a higher authority.'

'Charles?' said Karen derisively. 'I think you will find—'

'I have a higher authority than Charles.'

The line fell silent.

Sam seemingly sensed Karen's mind spinning with possible candidates.

'The prime minister?' she asked, finally.

'Pierre Bezukhov.'

'Um … Sorry … who?'

The line was silent again.

Sam clearly sensed a new doubt. Time to snuff it out once and for all. 'Pierre Bezukhov. He is the son of a Russian oligarch. He owns Dibble and Bains, as well as all the major publishing houses in Australia. He's socially awkward and kind, but he's not a man to anger. In his native Russia, he had a policeman tied to the back of a bear and thrown into a river.'

'Oh my,' said Karen. 'What happened to the policeman?'

'He nearly drowned, but Pierre was exiled to Australia.'

'Oh my,' said Karen again.

'He can literally either make you or cast you into the metaphorical river. Suffice to say, he's interested in your works. All these elaborate plans are his idea, and they are done with one aim in mind: to launch your career!'

'Yes, Mr Prufrock. I will do that, Mr Prufrock.'

'Remember, tell no one of this conversation or who instructed you to do this.'

'Yes, Mr Prufrock.'

'I'll call you in a week, Mrs Tiven. We'll go out for lunch to discuss money. I know this lovely place. A sawdust restaurant with oyster shells, where the women come and go, talking of Michelangelo.'

'It sounds very bohemian, Mr Prufrock. Let me guess. Is it in Carlton?'

'Yes. Now, Mrs Tiven, let me go make my visit.'

'Thank you, Mr Prufrock, and good luck with your question, I'm sure you'll get the response you seek. You're a very forthright gentleman.'

'I grow old. I grow old. I wear the bottom of my trousers rolled, Mrs Tiven.'

'Don't say that, Mr Prufrock. I'm sure you're still a distinguished gentleman.'

'Shall I part my hair behind? Do I dare to eat a peach? Shall I wear white flannel trousers and walk upon the beach?'

'If you're worried about the peach stains, then I suggest wearing darker-coloured pants.'

'Thank you, Mrs Tiven. I now have the strength to force the moment to its crisis.' Sam hung up the phone then called the offices of Dibble and Bains.

'Good to see people working on a Saturday. Is Sally Diamond there? No need to put her on, dear, I'm in a rush,' said Sam in his most feminine voice. 'Just tell her this is Yamparti Jones, and a Karen Tiven is dropping off the final proof for Ki Goonawanda's manuscript, *Dreamtime in Suburbia*. No need to call back.' Sam hung up.

It was done. There was nothing to do now but wait.

CHAPTER 21

A BUSINESS IDEA

All Saturday, with Sam shouting in my ear, I wrote with a maniacal intensity. My mood and intent personified by the wind and rain that lashed the windows and boxed the street tree branches into denuded arthritic stumps.

'Your three new rules for writing, Charles,' cried Sam. *'Are to write with passion in your heart, honesty in your mind, and cruelty in your veins.'*

I wrote three bare-boned stories stripped of adjectives, like the European street trees despoiled of their leaves. I spared no one. Not the people around me, not even myself. Hemmingway would have raised a mojito to my writing. I also fancied he would have disparaged me under his breath as he sipped his cocktail.

'No more sentimental mush!' shouted Sam. *'Passion, honesty, and most of all cruelty.'*

I carried on writing through the beeping of my mobile and then the knocking on the door and windows.

'Charles, are you home?' asked Nan outside. 'Charles? Are you taking your medication?'

I wanted to answer her. Open the door and let Nan come in. For me to wrap my arms around her and say, 'I'm in such trouble, Nan. Please help me. I think I've gone a bit far this time.'

But Sam disapproved of such a babyish and weak act.

I waited until she left, then continued writing. I didn't sleep at all that night, as I threw myself into my work.

Eugene was right. I was too naïve about the culture. Your worth as an individual now came down to the colour of your skin, your sexuality, your identity. What was important wasn't what you achieved or created, but your suffering and victimhood. The more exotic, the more oppressed your ancestors were, the greater your status in the culture. Victimhood, like the ace of spades, now trumped everything, even the content of your character.

Our society no longer venerated explorers and settlers. They were yesterday's men and women, tried, judged and condemned as sexist, racists, Anglo Saxon despoilers of the virgin earth. Destroyers of the pure and innocent Indigenous people, who before first contact lived in harmony with nature. More angels, than flawed and warlike humans.

Tear down the statues of these European rapist conquerors. Replace them with the new heroes of our society. The 'emoters'. They were the true heroes. People who leant into their identity and emoted all the slings and arrows of outrageous fortune they received. A cruel word here, a cruel word there, a perceived slight here, and a slight there. Dwell on it, stew on it, record it and finally shout! Shout! Let it all out over social media. Revel in your victim status. And if you don't have a sufficiently interesting identity, then create one. You, as the victim, are the hero. Meritocracy is dead! Long live identity!

I wrote this as an essay. Yamparti was right. We needed more politics in our literary magazines. I added another essay this time on Sam's three rules of writing.

With the first licks of the dawn on Monday morning, I reviewed what I had written over the weekend. My maniacal writing had produced enough fiction and essays for the third edition. I loaded them into the magazine maker and began editing furiously. After ensuring each story and essay was perfect, I sent the magazine layout to the printers, with instructions to start distributing as soon as next Friday.

Sam logged onto the *Imagine* website and all its social media accounts and changed the passwords.

I didn't go to the office on Monday or Tuesday. Instead, I changed tact and prepared for my important meeting at the Young and Jackson on Wednesday. By the early hours of Wednesday morning, I had completed the contract and was ready to face the world with my new business venture.

CHAPTER 22

COMMOTION IN THE OFFICE

Shouting and raised voices greeted Sam and me as we exited the elevator late on Wednesday morning.

'What were you thinking?'

'I was told to send the file to the printer.'

'Who told you? Who?'

Sam and I entered the office to find Yamparti leaning over Karen's desk, her nose and pointed finger almost in Karen's face.

'Who told you? Who?'

'I can't say,' said Karen.

Sam and I reclined onto our work chair and put our feet on our table.

'I demand to know who told you?' said Yamparti.

Karen sighed. 'All right, if you must know, it was the literary editor at Dibble and Bains.'

'Who? What editor?'

'J. Alfred Prufrock. He asked me to send the file to the printers and update the website.'

I couldn't see Yamparti's expression from where I sat. It was the only time in my life I regretted not seeing it.

'He rang me on Saturday morning and wanted me to send the file to the printers.'

'I see,' said Yamparti. 'You spoke to him on the phone?'

'Yes.'

'And where did he call from?'

'He called me from the street. He was off to ask a very important question and didn't have a lot of time.'

The ensuing unhinged laughter from Yamparti told me all I needed to know about her state of mind.

'Have you never heard of the poem, *Love Song of J. Alfred Prufrock*, by T.S. Eliot?'

'I'm not familiar with that song or artist.'

'My god! You ignoramus! J. Alfred Prufrock is a fictional character from a poem. You've been had, you stupid woman.'

'That's not true,' said Karen. 'I have a letter from him on Dibble and Bains' letterhead. He's going to publish my novels.'

'Publish your works?' cried Yamparti. 'No one in their right mind would publish your moronic psychobabble.'

'*Ouch*,' whispered Sam.

'That's wrong, I can prove to you that J. Alfred Prufrock is real. I have a letter from him.'

Yamparti dropped her head, and shaking it, she giggled hysterically.

'He's real. He works for Pierre Bezukhov, who runs all the major publishing houses in Australia.'

'Oh my god,' said Yamparti, her giggles turning to groans. 'Pierre Bezukhov is a character from *War and Peace*. You have heard of *War and Peace*?'

'I'm a busy woman, I can't keep up with all the latest foreign novels.'

'You fool. You hack,' said Yamparti. 'Someone has played you for all their worth and they …' She stopped mid-sentence. Her body straightened and stiffened.

'How dare you speak to me like that,' said Karen in the pause, sobbing. 'I demand an apology. I've had many compliments about my writing from many distinguished writers …'

Yamparti didn't respond to Karen's babble; instead, she turned slowly, pointing her finger in my direction. 'It was you,' she hissed slowly. 'You. You did this!'

I finally beheld her face, rigid, pale, with beads of sweat forming at her hairline. The pupils, in her wide, unblinking eyes, were like two cannon balls frozen in mid-air, seconds before falling upon a field of battle.

'You put Karen up to this.'

Before Sam's arrival, I would have cowered at this assault, dropped to my knees, and asked for forgiveness, promising to undertake the necessary struggle sessions to obtain forgiveness. But Sam's voice boomed in my head. *Write and speak with passion, honesty but most of all cruelty.* 'What … me?' I asked. 'Oh no, it wasn't me, but as for Sam, who knows what he's capable of.'

She leant over my desk, her face only inches from mine, her rancid breath like a slap on my nose. 'You've destroyed my reputation. I'm going to sue you for every last cent, Western. Every last cent.'

'Now, about your reputation,' said Sam. 'You didn't have any to begin with, so you won't get much in return.'

'This is the letter from Mr Prufrock,' cried Karen, waving the letter like Neville Chamberlain with his non-aggression pact.

Yamparti ripped the letter from Karen's grasp. She soon burst into hysterical laughter. 'It's fake. No one writes a letter like this. Can't you see you've been had?'

'You're lying.' Karen burst into tears. 'Mr Prufrock is real. Pierre Bezukhov is real. I won't tolerate people talking to me like this. I have a sick husband. I have mouths to feed.'

The phone rang.

Yamparti leapt on it, wrestling it from Karen's grasp.

'What! What!' shrieked Yamparti after a moment. 'I didn't leave a message with you … I said I didn't leave a message with you. A woman's voice. A woman's voice?' The light came on in Yamparti's eyes as she placed the phone to her chest. She glared at Karen then screamed, 'It was you!'

'What are you talking about?' asked Karen.

'I have Dibble and Bains on the line, and they said I called them on Saturday. You impersonated me.'

'Give me that phone,' said Karen. She wrestled it from Yamparti's grasp. 'Hello, this is Karen Tiven. I demand to speak to Mr Prufrock … Prufrock … I said Prufrock. It's J. Alfred Prufrock … That is J for Jackie, Alfred as in the hospital, then Prufrock. P for puppy. R for Robert. U for ukulele. F for frock … Yes … No … Yes … J. ALFRED PRUFROCK! He does work there. I spoke to him on Saturday, on the phone … No, he didn't leave a return number, he was in a rush to ask a very important question … No this is not a joke … No, I will not hand the phone back to Yamparti. I demand to speak to Pierre Bezukhov, then. That is Pierre, as in the French name, then B for Bob, E for elephant …' Karen sighed. 'He works there too. How can you not know him? He runs Dibble and Bains, and he wants to publish my writing. No, I will not hand back the phone to Yamparti, not until you put me through to Pierre.'

Eugene burst into the office, beetroot-faced, his neck veins bulging like the roots of a Moreton Bay fig tree. 'What have you done, Casper?' he said, leaning over my desk and pointing his finger in my face.

'It's Sam.'

'Stop with your imaginary friend nonsense.'

'So, you're a Sam-phobic.'

'I said stop with your nonsense. You changed my story. You've exposed me to the world.'

'Apart from a few word changes, it's the exact same story. Besides, someone needed to protect you, Eugene. Attacking the Catholic Church and the forces of conservatism, now that's career ending.'

'You heard him,' said Eugene, looking firstly at Yamparti then Karen. 'He's as good as admitted he changed the story.'

'Why are you so upset,' said Sam. 'You're famous. Look at all the publicity you'll get, especially with the Islamic community.'

'You've put me in physical danger!'

'Not at all,' I said. 'Islam is a religion of peace.'

'Yes, I can attest to that,' said Karen, finally off the phone, no doubt without any luck with Pierre or J. Alfred Prufrock.

We all turned to Karen.

'When I dropped off your novel at the Carlton Mosque,' said Karen, 'the man at the counter said the exact same words.'

Eugene's face turned from beetroot-red to onion-white, his mouth falling open. 'What. I don't understand. You did what?'

'J. Alfred Prufrock asked me to drop your novel off at the mosque. The man at the door was so kind and told me Islam was a peaceful religion, after I explained the novel was a gift from an up-and-coming Australian novelist.'

'What? I mean … You did what? J. Alfred Prufrock? What is happening?' Eugene turned towards Yamparti.

Yamparti, previously a ball of suppressed rage, visibly withered and tottered on her feet.

'You gave a copy of my edited novel to the Carlton Mosque?'

'They said they would read it.'

Eugene hyperventilated.

Yamparti tried to comfort him, but he pushed her aside. He seemed to be on the point of collapsing.

'Oh my god, I need to get to the mosque,' shouted Eugene, and he ran from the room, with Yamparti in tow.

The button on the elevator clattered like a shivering man in a snowstorm.

'Come on! Come on!' I heard Eugene repeat in quick succession before the fire door creaked open then closed with an echoing boom. The clattering footsteps of Eugene and Yamparti and their voices quickly receded into nothing.

Silence returned to the office.

I closed my eyes and smiled. My reverie was disturbed by several loud exhales.

Karen sat upright at her desk. With her eyes closed, she inhaled sharply, then extending both hands, as if undertaking a very, very slow tennis backhand, she exhaled loudly.

'What are you doing?' I asked. 'You look as if you're playing two-handed ping-pong.'

'I'm letting go of all Yamparti's negativity,' she said. 'It's a technique Laura taught me.'

'Yamparti was mean to you,' said Sam. 'Why don't you take the rest of the day off, as a paid mental health day. Maybe go speak to Laura. She might have an amulet to cure you of all negativities, for only nine ninety-nine.'

'I would rather stay.' She smiled.

'Hoping Mr Prufrock will call?'

Her smile said it all.

'I admire your faith,' said Sam. 'You just go on believing in him no matter what.'

'I will. I will,' she said, her eyes becoming misty like a windowpane on a winter's morning.

'Yamparti is a mean-tempered woman who's jealous of your writing skills,' said Sam. 'That's why she refuses to admit the existence of Mr Prufrock. It would mean conceding the superiority of your talent.'

'You know, Charles, I don't like to talk ill of another person—'

'I know, Karen, I know,' said Sam. 'It's the one thing I admire about you. Your forbearance in the face of other people's ignorance and meanness.'

'Yamparti shouldn't be managing staff. She doesn't know how to treat people. She hasn't experienced enough of the world, like I have.'

'I don't know how you put up with it?' Sam replied.

'Life is so tough sometimes,' said Karen. 'What, with all the troubles I face … a sick husband, kids with multiple personality issues—'

'Do you know where Boris is?' asked Sam, evidently tiring of Karen's chatter.

'He said he was booking a karaoke venue for his dad's group.'

Like Beetlejuice, Boris burst through the door, waving a piece of paper in the air. 'What's with this letter?' he demanded, looking pissed.

'You'll need to be more specific,' said Sam.

'This letter from you declining support for my manuscript.'

'As it says, we won't be supporting your endeavours to self-publish,' clarified Sam.

'I don't understand it,' said Boris. 'You loved the book, Charles.'

'Charles never liked the book,' said Sam. 'He only weakly supported you because you had a knife in your hand. I refuse to see Charles' money squandered on long, unedited, difficult to follow stories.'

Boris reddened. His hands curled into fists.

I would have cowered, but not Sam. He jumped to his feet and extended to his full height. 'If you're so certain of its success then why don't you organise a literary agent or a publisher, or get the money to publish it yourself?'

'Those people hate me. Besides, since my divorce, I can't organise finance,' whined Boris.

'We have come to an impasse then. You need Charles but Charles doesn't need you at all,' suggested Sam. 'Put the bloody thing up on Amazon yourself. You don't need any money to do that.'

'You don't understand, Charles. I need the capital to advertise it. Get it out in the marketplace and give myself the financial stability to write full-time.'

'The answer is no.'

Boris dropped to his knees, and then clasping his hands in prayer, he said, 'Charles, I beg you to reconsider. I'll do anything you ask.' Boris grabbed my leg, as Sam and I headed for the door. 'I'll even edit it!'

'Not even if you cut it in half,' said Sam.

Boris' bottom lip quivered; his eyes moistened. 'Help me, Charles. I know it's a bestseller. I just need the finance.'

Sam extracted me from the Serbian's grip, with a shake of my leg then a swift kick. 'Now, if you'll excuse me, I'm off to have a business meeting with a real author.'

CHAPTER 23

THE EROTIC TALES
OF KITTY WILD

'*B*oris' *idea is not a bad one,*' said Sam as we walked to our luncheon meeting. '*Find an up-and-coming author and invest money in getting them published.*'

'I'm worried about this,' I countered as we entered the Young and Jackson ten minutes before our luncheon meeting.

'*What's there to be worried about, Charles?*' asked Sam as we sat. '*I told you yesterday, self-publishing brokerage is the next big thing. We could be famous as the first person to think of it. Or second, but let's not consider Boris.*'

'I still don't like it,' I countered. 'How can we make it work?'

'*The key, Charles, is to start in a category that sells. Then select an author who writes well in that genre, perfect the business model in marketing and distribution, then sell lots and lots of books and split the profits with the author.*'

'But what genre sells?'

'*The same thing that sells everything, from cars to deodorant.*'

'And what is that?'

'*Sex, of course.*'

In the manuscripts and stories that flooded the offices of *Imagine* in its first weeks of existence, one stood out: *The Sorcerer's Slave,* by Kitty Wild. As its name suggested, it was a cross between magical fantasy and erotica. *Harry Potter* meets *Fifty Shades of Grey,* as the accompanying query letter described it.

It told the story of a young innocent witch, Lucinda Angel, who receives a scholarship to study at the Wizarding University of Romania. On her way, she is kidnapped by a group of black witches and taken to Hogtied Castle in the deepest, darkest Transylvania. If sex sold, then there were lashings of money to be made in Kitty Wild's tale.

What follows for Lucinda is a series of erotic adventures, with whips and broomsticks, and erotic dalliances with ghosts and ghouls, all overseen by a Macbethian council of witches. Lucinda is finally saved from her ordeal by a mysterious Snape-like wizard. She in turn saves him from his brooding introspection, and they live happily ever after, and conventionally sexually, one also hopes.

I had my doubts as to the appropriateness of the subject matter. What would Nan think? I blushed at the thought of her knowing I would be entering into a partnership with an author of erotic fiction. Even the idea of organising a business lunch with Kitty Wild caused my face to alight and my heart to race like a castanet player with ADHD.

Sam, of course, had no such scruples or fears. *'Don't you worry, Charles old boy, you let me manage things on your behalf.'*

Using my name, Sam had struck up a short correspondence with the author as soon as he took over the magazine. She sent another of her manuscripts to read. It had the even more suggestive title of *Whipped Cream.* This told the equally evocative story of young pastry chef Virginia True, who joins an exclusive boutique hotel in the country called 'The Castle', only to discover the clientele and the head chef have, how shall we say, exacting requirements they expect the staff and Virginia to fulfill. After reading it, I doubted many of the many sexual trysts described were anatomically possible. I also wondered whether

Chef Andre's use of vegetables from the cucurbits family would pass any local food-handling regulations.

I had my doubts as to the literary quality, but Sam saw Kitty Wild's money-making potential and set up the meeting under my name, hoping Kitty Wild would be our Dan Brown, or — dare I hoped — our J.K. Rowling of the Marquis de Sade variety.

As Sam and I waited for our modern-day Pauline Réage to arrive, I fell into one of my favourite reveries over the last few days, in imagining Kitty Wild. I pictured that Kitty was in her early forties, still beautiful, but in a faded glamorous way, like a sinuous Rita Hayworth-styled redhead, seated cross-legged at the bar in a black dress cut at the side, exposing her long, smooth legs. She sat chain-smoking and sipping her whiskey sour as she spoke to me in a world-weary, suggestive and husky voice, of the many love affairs she had had and would have.

Her name and writing had certainly fired my male brain. Late at night, with nothing better to do, and trying to forget Celeste for a time, I slowly created my imagined Kitty Wild.

Using Google images as my source, I created a photoshop image of Kitty, using the hair and body of Rita Hayworth, mixing it with Gigi Hadid's eyes, and Nicole Kidman's forehead. To cool my overheated imagination and not spoil my burgeoning love for Celeste, I gave my Kitty the nose and cheeks of Julia Gillard, Nan's least favourite ex-prime minister.

'What is it with that voice,' Nan often said, whenever she came on the television. 'It is so false. So contrived. No one in Adelaide speaks like that. Why can't she speak like a proper prime minister, like Bob Menzies or John Howard.'

Caught up in this reverie, I failed to heed the little old lady with a knitting bag, standing next to me.

'Excuse me, are you Charles Western?'

'Pardon?'

'Are you Charles Western?'

'Yes,' I said, rising to my feet.

'I'm Kitty Wild. Or that is my nom de plume. My real name is Mary White, how do you do?'

Mary White, a short grey-haired woman with a wrinkled forehead examined me with inquisitive and intelligent hazel eyes over the rims of her glasses. I guessed her north of seventy.

'You're Kitty Wild?' I said, unable to keep the surprise from my voice and face. 'I was expecting … someone …' I stopped there.

'Younger,' she said, completing the sentence.

Heat rose up my neck, and I nodded as she sat in the seat I offered.

'Don't be embarrassed, I must confess that I expected you to be older. You don't look like a publisher.'

We ordered our meals, and after the waiter took away the menus, I asked the question burning on the tip of my tongue, like the many hot pokers on Lucinda's body.

'What got you into writing?' I really wanted to ask: 'why erotic fiction', but I thought I could lead up to the question slowly, unlike the sex in her stories.

'I started writing soon after Ted, my husband, passed away. We were married forty-two happy years. With the children having left home many years before, I found myself all alone with nothing to do. I had my knitting group, and the local church where I worked every Sunday in the café, and of course, looking after the grandchildren from time to time, but not enough to fill all my spare time. I had always dabbled in fiction, writing a few romantic Mills and Boon stories earlier in my life. I started writing these again after Ted's death and tried to get them published. It was while I was in a second-hand bookstore that I stumbled across an erotic fantasy novel: *After Midnight.* A terrible story. I knew immediately I could write better, and so I changed genre. I always enjoyed the challenge of writing sex scenes in romantic tales, so I took to the erotic genre with glee. I've been writing erotic fiction now for the last five years, usually after church on Sunday.' Mary stopped speaking and eyed me over the rims of her glasses. 'Why are you blushing dear, is there anything wrong?'

'I was just thinking of you writing erotic fiction after church.'

'Funny you should mention that. For all my books, I spend considerable time researching before I start writing. For *The Sorcerers Slave*, I spent several Saturday nights in a dungeon in the city, researching various bondage techniques. One of the slaves, sorry ... I should say "clientele", happened to be my Anglican minister.'

I spat out my Caesar salad and coughed uncontrollably.

'Would you like some water, dear?'

'No. No. One of the anchovies went down funny, that's all. They are very bitter.'

'Funny you should say bitter. As Minister Giles was whipped, he kept reciting Act 8:23 repeatedly. In the gall of bitterness and in the bondage of iniquity, spank me!'

My head ignited with warmth, and I downed the rest of my beer. I realised it was hot in the Young and Jackson. Very hot.

'Now, I understand why he was so obsessed about the Book of Exodus,' continued Mary, more to herself than me. 'He also quoted a lot from Deuteronomy in his sermons. "And the Egyptians' evil entreated us, and afflicted us, and laid upon us hard bondage." That was another of his favourite passages. It goes to show, one cannot judge a book by its cover. Though you can judge a minister by his choice of scripture.'

We ate our main meal in silence for a time.

I was stunned. Mary, with a wry smile on her face, seemed to be contemplating her minister. I thought it best to let Sam take the lead.

He pushed away our Caesar salad and started. 'We want to enter into a business partnership with you, Kitty, I mean, Mary,' he said. 'We have an eye for literary talent and believe you are the next best thing in the

Australian literary scene. We want to help you reach your potential.'

'How?' she asked.

'We want to finance the publication of *The Sorcerer's Slave*. Pay for copyediting, proofreading, advertising, book layout, and cover design, as well as all costs associated with uploading onto distribution platforms, such as Amazon, which we'll set up under our venture's name. Then once our initial investment is paid off, we'd then split the profits fifty-fifty.'

'You're a micro-investor?'

'We call it a "literary brokerage service", and you're the big winner, Mary. You don't need to pay any upfront costs. We do it all for you.'

'How is this different from a normal publishing business?'

'Firstly, we don't have any overheads, like a traditional publishing house. All the functions, book layouts, cover design, and marketing are outsourced. The entire venture will be online.'

'How will you market the book?'

'We intend to go wide on all platforms, including audio. As part of the deal, we want you to do the narration. We'll assist as part of this process. We'll also advertise on BookBub, Facebook, and Amazon. It's all in the contract.'

'Contract?'

Sam took from the bag, a typed contract and handed it to Mary. It was based on Boris' *Terror at the Airport* contract but heavily edited and changed, as Sam and I thought through all the permutations of our new business venture.

'As you can see on the last page, it has a fifty-fifty split in profits after Write Creative Press Pty Ltd, that is our company, recoups all upfront costs. What this means, Mary, is you can concentrate on your novels, knowing you will be published and marketed, while retaining complete artistic freedom of your works. You won't lose anything financially from the deal. We're the ones taking all the risks. We intend to publish a range of high- and low-content books under the Write Creative Press label. You'll be our first author, Mary, in the high-content book range.'

'You use "our" and "we" quite are lot. Are you talking about the company, or is this an unusual use of pronouns that you young people seem to be fond of using these days?'

I sat forward. 'No. No, I have a silent partner called Sam. He was the one who suggested this idea, as well as drafted the contract?'

'I must say, I'm very impressed with the work and thought that you've put into this venture of yours.'

I smiled.

'But I'll need time to think this offer through.'

'Take all the time you need.'

'Now, if you'll excuse me,' said Mary, 'I'm off to the afternoon shift at Kittens.'

'Kittens?' I blushed and looked wide-eyed in amazement at Mary.

Mary obviously read my mind. 'Research, dear. Research. Good lord, dear boy, I'm far too old for any hanky panky.'

'Sorry.'

'Give me a nice cup of tea and a crime thriller any day. No, the establishment lets me sit in the tearoom and interview the girls between sessions with clients. It's for my next book. I've brought my knitting,' she said, lifting the bag she carried. 'I'm told it will be a slow afternoon.'

'Do you have a working title yet of this new manuscript?'

'No, but how does this sound for the back cover. Millionaire surgeon by day, bloodsucking vampire by night.'

'I'm afraid vampires are not in vogue anymore.'

'They will come back in fashion … literary tastes, like everything else, go in cycles, and when it comes back, I'll be ready with the book.'

'Well then, I'll be ready to help you publish it, Mary.'

'Let me think about your offer, dear; and thank you for the lunch. Now, if you'll excuse me. I must go.'

CHAPTER 24

NAN AND THE NEWSPAPERS

After Mary left, I ordered another beer then sat in the warm glow of my triumphal meeting. Sam spoke with confidence and authority. I went over in my mind the new business model. Sam would fire Yamparti, Boris and Karen, and replace them with real writers. No more Mr Nice Charles Western at work, but cruel and ruthless Sam.

The magazine would only be the tip of a publishing empire comprising low-content books: calendars, diaries, and puzzle books. Mary would be the start of the high-content roster of books to be published. I already imagined Write Creative Press' erotic range.

I burst out laughing at the absurdity of my own preconceived notions about Kitty Wild. I was laughing so hard that others in the room stopped what they were doing to look my way.

My mobile rang, and I made the mistake of answering it.

'Charles, thank god it's you. It's Nan.'

I sighed, realising I hadn't returned any of her calls or replied to any of the notes shoved under my door at home.

'We need to talk urgently.'

'Why?'

'The newspapers are writing stories about you?'

'What?'

'I didn't believe it myself when Terry Smith first told me, but I've gone online, and they are writing articles about you.'

'What newspapers? What articles?'

'All of them. *The Age*, the *Herald Sun*, the *Daily Mail*.'

'What are they saying?'

'That your magazine is spreading hateful messaging on university campuses. That you've changed stories to defame two people, one was an ex-prefect at Victoria Grammar. And that you're mad.'

'It's all lies, Nan.'

'And who is this Sam?'

'He's someone I've employed to help me run the magazine.'

'Well, I don't like him. I don't like him at all. He's leading my grandson astray.'

'He's a perfectly respectable young man,' I said.

'I want you to get out of this literary business. All the people in it are awful. I want you to get into a nice profession, such as law or medicine.'

'I like what I do.'

'I'm ringing the journalists to stop them spreading lies about you.'

'No, Nan, please don't. They'll only use what you say to further twist the truth.'

'But I don't like what they're saying about my grandson.'

'Just promise me you won't call the papers, Nan. You'll only pour more fuel on the fire.'

'Well, you can't stop me from inviting Mr Jefferies to dinner tomorrow night. You know Mr Jefferies, from our church. He's a solicitor, and I want you to come too, Charles. I want to see what legal options we have.'

From the corner of my mind, Sam waved his arms, wanting to take the phone.

'We can't let them defame you, Charles.'

'Don't worry, Nan, it'll all blow over.'

'I can't help but worry, Charles, I really don't want you mixed up with all these literary people. They're spiteful, always taking offence at the most trivial, ridiculous things, and always starting feuds. Also, I want you to see Dr Regi again. I'm worried you're not taking your medication. Charles, are you taking your medication? Charles? Charles?'

Sam pulled at my hand gripping the mobile. *'You know she'll be badgering you about this for weeks, if not months,'* he whispered. *'Let me speak to her. I know how to stop her obsessing on the articles, threatened court action and your medication.'*

'All these writers do all day, Charles, is live off the taxpayer, sleep around and sue one another. Now they're going to sue my grandson. I can't let them do that …'

I handed the mobile to Sam.

'Mrs Whitechapel. This is Sam. Just letting you know that Charles is dating a French exchange student. He's head over heels in love with her. Also, he's going to use his money to fund the publications of Kitty Wild's explicit erotic novels. One is called *Whipped Cream*, and the other is called *The Sorcerer's Slave*. We love you, bye,' Sam rang off.

'That should stop her obsessing over the newspaper articles,' said Sam. *'Now, let's fire up the laptop. I want to see what these devils are writing about us.'*

We ordered another beer and turned on the laptop.

It didn't take long to find the first article in our social media feed.

Heir to Western Discount Chain spreading hate across University Campuses, screamed the headline from *The Age*. It was accompanied by a photo of me in my Victoria Grammar blazer.

'An old journalistic staple,' said Sam. *'The "private schoolboy gone bad" narrative. But how did they get the photo?'*

'They work quick,' I retorted.

The article started:

New literary magazine, *Imagine*, founded by Charles Western, son of discount chain king, Doug Western, is accused of spreading hate speech across several university campuses in Melbourne. Spokesperson for The Coalition of Muslims and Permanently Outraged Transgender Students (COMPOST) has accused the new magazine of inciting violence against Islamic and transgender students and has called for the universities to strengthen hate speech laws. 'Universities should be a safe space from this type of hate, rather than spreading it,' the spokesperson added.

Yamparti Jones, the editor for the magazine, denied any responsibility for the edition. When pressed on the changes, she said, 'The edition was changed without my knowledge or consent. All references to Christianity were swapped with Islam, and the word 'men' was changed to 'women'. Also, an unapproved article disparaging female and transwomen was added without my consent, under my by-line.'

A spokeswoman for the magazine, Karen Tiven said, 'Changes to the magazine were approved by Russian Oligarch Pierre Bezukhov. He is a big player in the Australian publishing scene, though he likes this to remain a secret. He will be publishing all my novels soon.

Those close to the magazine say that with the arrival of a shadowy figure called Sam, the magazine has gone in a radically right-wing direction.

A similar article to *The Age* appeared in the *Herald Sun*. The *Daily Mail* also ran the following article: *Australian Author Apologises to Islamic and Indigenous Communities.*

The article started:

Up-and-coming author Eugene Whiteford, son of Labour advisor Archie Whiteford, has unreservedly apologised to the Islamic and Indigenous communities after the first chapter of his upcoming novel *Dreamtime in Suburbia* was featured in the controversial right-wing literary magazine, *Imagine.*

Mr Whiteford, writing under the penned name of Ki Goonawanda, has set *Dreamtime in Suburbia* in a dystopian future, involving a Muslim prime minister who suspends democracy and orders the murder of Jewish refugees. The novel has drawn widespread criticism from Muslim groups for its depiction of the Islamic community.

'The owner of the magazine changed key words in my novel,' said Mr Whiteford in a statement to the *Daily Mail.* 'My novel was supposed to be a critique on the Catholic Church, but the word Catholic was changed to the word Muslim.'

Mr Whiteford, who attended the exclusive Victoria Grammar, also drew fire from Indigenous groups for the use of the pen name Ki Goonawanda, many assuming the author to be of Indigenous descent.

'I understand many may mistake my motives in using this nom de plume,' added Mr Whiteford. 'I never attempted to appropriate another culture for my own purposes. My intention was merely to empower Indigenous voices.'

Publishers Dibble and Bains, who were set to publish the manuscript in the spring, have dropped the book after the backlash. A spokesperson for Dibble and Bains, Sally Diamond said, 'Our number one priority is furthering civil discourse within society. Stories that seek to denigrate marginalised communities have no place on our roster.'

'Ouch,' said Sam. *'Me thinks Eugene is in big trouble now.'*

After reading the articles, I checked my mobile. It had been ringing and beeping constantly throughout lunch, and now as I poured through the articles, I thought it might spin and vibrate off the table and out the door.

On top of the unread messages from Nan on the weekend, I had a further thirty-five voice messages: four from journalists wanting comment, one from Eugene: 'I'm going to sue you, Casper, for every cent you own!' Another from Yamparti, which consisted in a long, loud scream. At least five from Boris were begging me to reconsider my decision not to fund his book, with five accompanying begging text messages.

The rest came from Nan, who thankfully was no longer obsessing about the papers, or medications, but now my love life and immortal soul.

2.15: 'Charles, please call me as soon as you receive this message. We need to discuss this librarian Kitty.'

2.20: 'Charles, when am I going to meet Kitty. I hope she speaks English. Will I need to buy a French phrasebook?'

2.32: 'Charles, where did you meet this Kitty? I hope you're staying away from the gentlemen clubs in the city. Charles, please call me back at once.'

2.35: 'Charles, this is your nan. I don't want you involved in pornography. You know it is bad for the soul.'

2.54: 'Charles, it's your nan again. Please come tomorrow night to dinner. As well as Mr Jefferies, I've invited the new minister at church, Reverend Giles. He's only just joined the parish. You'll like him. He's a leading authority on the Jewish captivity in Egypt.'

2.56: 'Does Kitty like roast? Why don't you bring her to dinner tomorrow night also. Reverend Giles is keen to meet you both.'

2.58: 'Charles, I'm worried about you and this Kitty. I don't know whether I approve of you dating an escort, especially a French one.'

3.15: 'Charles, I've just spoken to the Reverend Giles. He suggests reciting Act 8:23 before going to bed.'

I decided to deal with Nan's muddled grasp of Sam's message later. Sam had been tugging for the phone for some time, wanting sport. He eventually took the mobile and first dealt with the annoying Boris.

Sam texted: `What part of the word NO do you not understand?`

Instantly, the phone beeped back with Boris' reply: `You're the last hope for the project.`

Sam texted: `NOOOOOOOOOOOOOOOOOOOOOOOOOOOOO.`

Boris texted back: `Okay. Prepared to change airport scenario. Please reconsider funding.`

Sam then said to me, '*Well, that sounds sincere. Maybe his book could sell? With all this talk of Russian oligarchs, we can cash in. Let's back Boris.*'

'You're not serious?' I asked.

'*You're right, I'm not.*' Sam laughed. '*But it's good to string him along a little longer. Think of it as dangling a plastic mouse on the end of a string, and Boris as an enormously genetically engineered kitten.*'

Sam texted Boris: `Yes, to Russian special forces and Dr Sidrov entanglement bomb; drop everything else.`

A text appeared thirty seconds later: `Want to keep Indonesian-Chinese Invasion as part of the mix.`

Sam texted: `No.`

Boris replied, a minute later: `Okay, boss. Can I get an advance on my money?`

`Not until job is done,` Sam texted back.

`But how can I do the job without funds?`

`You're a big boy,` texted Sam. `You'll find a way.`

'You're going to make him do all that editing then not accept it?' I asked.

Sam's smile in the reflection of the window said all I needed to know.

'That gives me an idea about our Kitty Wild slash Mary White,' said Sam. On the laptop, Sam brought up her last email and wrote: `Dear Kitty. Replace millionaire surgeon with a foreign spy. Also suggest changing your name to Roxanne Wild.`

'Why Roxanne?' I said, but then I remembered the eighties song, 'Roxanne' by The Police.

`Also, what do you think of this as Roxanne Wild?` wrote Sam, attaching my photoshopped picture of Kitty and hitting send. *'Right, now the journos,'* said Sam.

He started with Sally Twist from *The Guardian*.

'Hello, Sally, this is Sam calling on behalf of Charles Western.'

'I'm after Charles Western,' said Sally.

'You will need to speak to me. I handle all of Charles' business affairs.'

'Really. And how long have you been managing his affairs, Sam?'

'A couple of weeks. We met on Swanston Street Bridge.'

'Was this an arranged meeting?'

'Not at all. It was a chance one.'

'What is your last name?'

'My name is just Sam. My controller gave me no last name.'

'Your ... what?'

'My controller. I'm an invention. A figment of the imagination.'

'Would that be of Pierre Bez ... Bezuk ...'

'Bezukhov, Sally.'

'Yes.'

'Are you wondering whether he created me? Let us say, Sally, we're drawn from the same imaginative ether. Sally, do you sense the imaginative ether all around you?'

'Excuse me?'

'Interesting fact, Sally ... did you know that Pierre Bezukhov's handler worked as an artillery officer in the Crimea?'

'Pierre is handled by the Red Army?' she asked.

'Tsarist, Red Army. I prefer the Russian Army, Sally.'

'I see. I see. Now, coming back to the magazine. Are you and Pierre running the magazine?'

'Running is too strong a word. I like guiding, shaping, moulding. Between you and me, Sally, Charles is a sweet young man, but too soft. I'm here to be his enforcer.'

'So, you and Pierre set the editorial content of the magazine, and Charles Western is the front?'

'No, our editor Yamparti sets the editorial content. She likes Russia too.' Sam gave me the thumbs up in the window reflection as we listened to Sally type on the other end.

'What are you doing?' I cried, snatching away the phone and hanging up.

'*Having fun,*' said Sam.

Several patrons who walked into the bar stopped to stare open-mouthed at us arguing. I had noticed through my heated exchanges with Sam, the general chatter of the bar had halted, and many eyes were now focusing on us.

The phone rang again then went to voice mail.

Sally proposed a sit-down interview.

Sam then rang *The Age* journalist next.

'Listen, Peter, I don't have much time,' said Sam as soon as Peter answered. 'I've uncovered a plot to overthrow a crazy socialist state government with an even crazier one. If there is one name you need to remember from this phone call, it's Boris. Boris Petrović. He is an antisemite preparing the ground for a joint Chinese–Indonesian invasion of Australia.'

'Excuse me?'

'Excuses won't be tolerated in the new Australia, if Boris has his way.'

The phone went dead.

I called again.

'Hello.'

'This is the managing director of *Imagine* magazine. I'm returning your call.'

'Oh good. Sorry, I just got off the phone with a crazy person.'

'I sympathise with you. The world is full of crazy people … Now, how can I help you?'

'Do you have any comment about the latest edition of your magazine.'

Sam grabbed the phone from my hands and started speaking. 'Only a few nouns were changed in each article to better reflect the intention of the authors. Also, Charles is deeply committed to standing up for the oppressed and marginalised in our society.'

'So, Charles is committed to refugees and the Indigenous?' asked the journalist.

'No,' cried Sam. 'Far more marginalised people than that. I'm talking about white Anglo Saxon young men from elite private schools. They can't even get a book deal unless they pretend to be Aboriginal or someone from an oppressed intersectional community. Do you think that's fair, Peter? Do you?'

'Um, are you the guy I was talking to before on the phone?'

'Charles and I are striking a blow for Eugene Whiteford and all the young men like him. Did you know he went to Victoria Grammar and was a prefect? I can send photos of him in his cadet uniform.'

The phone went dead a second time.

Sam called the *Daily Mail* journalist next. 'Hi, this is Sam, you left a message, Misha?'

'Sorry. Who is this?' asked Misha.

'Exactly? You rang Charles Western.'

'Yes, and your name again?'

'Sam.'

'Sam, who?'

'Exactly.'

'Sam, who?'

'Exactly.'

The line fell silent.

Sam and I could sense the little cogs of her mind ticking around and around, making other bigger cogs click into life, forming mental notes, suggestions, which folded into preconceived narratives.

'Did you know, Misha, Eugene went to Victoria Grammar and was a prefect? I can send photos of him in a kilt if you want?'

'That would be great. Now, can Charles Western give a comment about the latest edition of *Imagine*?'

'I handle all his dealings with the press.'

'How do you spell your last name, Sam?'

'My name is Sam.'

'You said it was Sam, but Sam who?'

'Exactly, that is the question.'

The line fell silent.

Charles and I sensed the same cogs spinning around and around and around like an automata clockwork figure.

'Um ... Chinese?'

'Did you know a fellow in my employee is organising a Chinese–Indonesian invasion.'

'Excuse me?' Misha replied.

'I asked him to cut it, but he won't. It's all an intricate CIA plot.'

'Sorry?'

'Stop apologising.'

'Um.'

I took the phone from Sam's grasp and hung up.

'You need to stop this,' I scolded Sam. 'No more calls.' I switched off the mobile and buried it deep in my pocket, away from the clutches of Sam. I suddenly felt cold and very afraid, realising Sam would say and do anything.

'Relax, Charlie boy, this will all blow over in a few days. Besides, it's great marketing for the magazine. Think of all the advertising revenue you can charge.'

'Listen, I don't want you around for the next few hours, Sam,' I said. 'Tonight, I'm taking Celeste out, and I don't want you talking. I want you to keep your head down and your comments to yourself.'

'Fine, but if you fail, as I'm sure you will, then I get to take her out.'

'I won't fail. But it is a deal,' I said, rising to my feet and metaphorically shaking his hand. I packed up my laptop, turned and headed out the exit, conscious of the many squinting eyes and opened mouths watching us pass into the street.

CHAPTER 25

ENGLISH CUISINE AT ITS FINEST

I met Celeste, without Sam, outside Luna Park at five pm.

'Where are you taking me?' she asked.

'Tonight, we're going to dine on the finest English cuisine.'

Celeste smiled, but her eyes clouded with incomprehension.

On Acland Street, I ordered us two pieces of flake, four potato cakes, chips for two, and four dim sims all wrapped in butcher's paper. To wash down this mouth-watering delicacy, I bought two cans of Fanta. For dessert, I procured a treat of two Caramello Koalas from a nearby newsagent.

On the grass near St Kilda pier, we unrolled our food, and waving away the gathering flock of bad-tempered seagulls, we ate our dinner. The cool, cloudless day, turning into a cold evening as the sun, like a cough drop, was swallowed by the bay. I took off my jacket and placed it on Celeste's shoulders, feeling for the first time in days, at peace. My heart not racing clackety clack; Sam not shouting in my head. My mobile, with its hundreds of messages, was now turned off and buried deep in my pocket, out of reach from Sam. Yamparti and Eugene momentarily forgotten. The outcry in the newspapers seemed so far, far away. I was here on this beautiful clear, but cool night with a girl I loved, in a quiet spot by the edge of the bay.

'Thank you.' She beamed as she readjusted my jacket.

'So, how do you like the finest offering of English cuisine?' I asked.

'It's lovely,' she said. 'But what is this?'

'A dim sim. It's the Australian addition to the traditional English fare of fish and chips.'

'What's it made of?'

'I'm sorry, that's a state secret,' I said. 'And I'd need to kill you if I told you.'

Celeste laughed before taking a bite. 'It's bitter,' she said.

I smiled and wondered whether I should tell Celeste about Mary White and her Anglican minister. Better not. It would only get lost in translation. And besides, how would I explain my intent to publish her erotic fiction. Would she think me perverted? Instead, I raised my can of Fanta. 'To English cuisine.'

We clinked our cans and ate in silence as a tanker left Port Melbourne for the Heads. About us, a chorus of seagulls haggled and grunted for our dinner. Celeste threw a chip, and a seagull melee ensued at our feet, attracting more of these silver scavengers ready for the leftovers.

After eating my Caramello Koala, I rolled onto my side and studied Celeste's face as she ate. I was captivated by her beauty. The way her eyes twinkled with amusement as she fed the last of her chips to the hungry avian hordes. Finally, wiping her hands to prove to the seagulls she had nothing left, she lay back down on the grass, and turning her gaze to me, she asked. 'Why did you create a magazine, Charles?'

I didn't answer at first. Instead, I studied Celeste's eyes, now only centimetres from mine. I had been asked this question so many times over the last few months, and each time I gave some hazy answer. I realised as I examined her closely, who Celeste reminded me of and why I found her so attractive: my mother. Not so much in looks but in personality. Or the personality I had drawn of my mother from my many conversations with Nan. I had built a picture of a sweet-natured, caring, but also cultured, and no doubt brilliant woman.

'Maybe I created the magazine,' I finally said, 'not only as a way of creating something as big and important as my father, but as a way of honouring my mother.' I took a deep breath as a wave of sadness, like a sudden large wave crashing to shore, washed over me. 'There isn't a day when I don't think of her.' I sniffled. My god, I was about to cry again. I couldn't let Celeste see me cry. I took another deep breath and thought of the tidal forecasts for Port Phillip Bay. That did it. 'Now I have a question for you,' I said.

'You're trying to change the subject,' she said.

'Shamelessly,' I replied. 'I want this dinner to be about you, Celeste. I want to know everything there is to know about you.'

She smiled.

'What do you want out of this one and only life?' I asked. 'Do you have any goals?'

'Like what?' asked Celeste, still staring into my eyes.

'I don't know, do you want to become a world-famous psychologist. Discovering some cure to a neurosis.'

Celeste threw back her head and laughed.

I considered then becoming a comedian just so I could hear her laugh repeatedly.

Celeste rolled onto her back, and looking up at the few stars visible, she said. 'I don't want fame or money or a big house. All I want is a simple life, filled with simple pleasures, like laughter and music, or looking out from a cosy room onto a garden on a rainy winter's day all snug and warm by a fire. I want to wander outside in the sunshine in summer, feeling the cool green grass through my toes. I want a life filled with love.' She rolled onto her side and looked at me. 'A life I can share with someone special. Someone I can share my heart, my mind and soul with. Someone I can walk along the beach and eat fish and chips by the water's edge with.'

My gaze was trapped in the gravitational pull of her eyes. I could go on staring into hers for eternity. I was her prisoner. A willing captive. I could go on examining each of her delicate and slender eyelashes, mapping the smooth creaminess of her skin, marvelling at the sculptured manicure of her eyebrows. So absorbed by her magnetic allure, I failed to hear her voice …

'Charles. Charles.'

'Sorry … what?'

'What do you want out of life?'

I sighed and turned to lie on my back to look up at one of the few stars strong enough to penetrate the light haze of Melbourne. I sensed her almond eyes studying my features whimsically, like a snatch of Debussy. 'All my life, I've wanted to create something so beautiful that it stops the world,' I said, surprised at my own words, which poured into my soul from somewhere outside of myself. As if imbibed from the starlight falling from this one visible celestial object, and I had now reassembled it into words. 'I want to create something so beautiful, whether it be a story, a poem, a gesture, an act, or through loving someone. I want to create something that enchants the ear, bewitches the eye, intoxicates the nose. I want to create something people go back to again and again. I want to create a world of beauty.'

With a sudden insight, I realised that that was what I wanted to do with *Imagine*. That was my goal. My real intention before it became polluted by the agendas of Boris, Yamparti, Karen, and most of all Sam. I had let my own cowardness betray my true intent.

I rolled onto my side again and stared into Celeste's eyes, making out the subtle changes in hue between each pigmented ring of her irises. My cheeks tingling with the caress of her breath on my face. 'I want to create something as beautiful as you, Celeste.'

We stared into each other's eyes. My face was drawing towards hers slowly. Yet the closer my lips crept, a nagging doubt took hold. A voice like Sam's, like Raven's boomed in my head. *You're not good enough. You're not tall, witty, smart, or happy enough for her. Good god, boy, you failed your VCE, how can you take care of a girl like Celeste? She needs a man who is more psychologically stable. You're weak, boy! Weak!*

'What is it, Charles?' she said as I drew away and sat up eyeing the horizon on the bay.

'It's late Celeste and cold. I should take you home.'

CHAPTER 26

THE UNEXPECTED GUEST

I took a surprised Celeste back to her lodgings in North Melbourne, shaking her hand at her front door. After she went inside, I wandered down the street, stopping at the corner to bang my head against a brick wall. I beat my head so hard against the rough surface, I left a bruise on my forehead.

'Are you all right, mate?' a passing man asked.

But I went on beating my head on the wall, and the man — no doubt thinking me just another deranged vagrant all big cities possess — finally went on his way.

'What was I thinking?' I screamed, beating the brick surface with my fist now. 'I could have kissed her. I could have kissed her ... and what do I do? I go and shake her hand.'

'*Self-sabotage again, Charles. You're so pathetic. You let the Raven get to you,*' said Sam. '*As for nearly crying in front of her. What were you thinking? Women say they want men to express their emotions, but that's a lie. They want a man who is stoic, who can throw a dead pig over his shoulder and bring home the bacon. You leave her to me. I'll take care of your love life, like I'm doing with your magazine.*'

'No.' I whipped out my phone.

'*What are you doing?*' asked Sam.

'I'm calling her up. I want to take her out again.'

'No,' said Sam. '*We made a deal. You had your chance, it's my turn now. I know what women want. They like a man who is exciting, daring and dangerous. One who is prepared to shower them with gifts, take them to fancy restaurants and exotic locations. You leave the next date to me. I will have her wrapped around our fingers in no time.*'

'Then at least let me call Nan to sort out the mess with your last message.'

'*Don't do anything of the sort,*' said Sam. '*Are you going to be a snivelling little boy for the rest of your life; always worrying what others think about you? Let her think what she wants. You're your own man, now.*'

Sam organised an Uber, and as we waited, I flicked through the phone. Another thirty voice messages awaited my reply. Fifteen from Nan, several from journalists, and the rest from Boris begging for an advance.

Our Uber pulled up, and I got in the back seat.

'Hello, sir, my name is Raj.'

'Hello,' I said.

We drove in silence for a time, before Raj looked at me through the rear-vision mirror and said, 'You look sad, sir.'

'Women troubles.'

'Ah well, sir, if you're looking for a woman, I can introduce you to my cousin Atfah. She is in her last year of medicine at Monash. She is dutiful and pretty and is also looking to stay in Australia and—'

'Thanks kindly, but I like the girl I'm seeing.'

'Well, if that is the case and you want to forget your troubles, I can take you to some wonderful night spots in Melbourne. Places where the beer is fresh and the women very nice and attentive.'

'Thank you, but I'd rather go home and pound my head softly on a wall.'

'If you wish, sir.'

I texted Celeste before Sam could berate me: `Dinner next Friday night? I'll tell you the state secret for dim sim. Be ready around seven.`

Almost immediately, Boris texted back: `That would be good. We can discuss my advance over dinner.`

I didn't bother replying to Boris that I had texted him by mistake.

Instead, Sam took over the phone and texted Celeste: `Date next Friday. Be ready at seven. Love Sam.`

'Here you are, sir.'

We had pulled up outside my flat.

'Do you have a card with your mobile, Raj?'

'Why yes,' he said, pulling one from his pocket.

'Do you do private assignments?'

'I'm busy studying—'

'I'll pay for a full night plus five hundred on top.'

'When do you want me?'

'I'll call you.'

'I didn't catch your name, sir.'

'Sam. My name is Sam.'

After Raj left, I opened the gate to my modest abode. Two letters in Nan's handwriting greeted me on my welcome mat. Sam threw them in the recycling bin before opening the front door. After taking a few steps inside, we jumped back in fright.

A man sat on my couch eating yogurt. I grabbed the first large menacing object I could find, my Nimbus 2000 straw broom, which I had bought on eBay during lockdown. Lifting it high over my head, I cried. 'Who are you and what are you doing in my apartment?'

'Aren't you supposed to fly that, instead of using it as a weapon?' said the man unfazed.'

'Who are you?' I repeated, my Nimbus 2000 ready to strike.

The man in his early thirties sighed, put down the yogurt and spoon and took from his pocket a badge. 'Special Officer Daniel Oberon from Australian Security Intelligence Organisation. ASIO for short.'

I edged forward slowly, and with the Nimbus 2000 still raised over my head, I eyed the badge. 'How did you get in, and why are you eating my yogurt?'

'Your nan has been knocking on your door for the last hour. She has only just left. She's very worried about you.'

'I asked, how did you get in, and why are you eating my yogurt?'

'I'm a Spook, and your security isn't all that crash hot. In future, I'd lock your windows. As for the yogurt, sorry about that. You took longer than expected, and I hadn't had dinner. I hope you don't mind. ASIO will reimburse you for it.'

'Never mind the yogurt. I want you out of my apartment.'

'First, we need to discuss Sam Woo.'

'Who?'

'Exactly. Woo. How long have you been working with Chinese intelligence?'

'Sam? Sam who?' I shook my head. 'What the hell are you talking about?' Then the light came on. 'OH ...'

'We have reason to believe Sam Woo is a Chinese operative sent to infiltrate the right-wing media.'

'There is no Sam Woo,' I said, putting down the Nimbus 2000.

'We have the text message you sent one of your operatives, Kitty Wild. "Replace millionaire surgeon with foreign spy." Is that what you're doing with Chinese security, infiltrating the Australian medical sector for intellectual property, as well as the media to stoke unrest, then taking a cut of the action?'

'You're reading my text messages? That's an invasion of privacy, not to mention illegal."

'Oh, you're so naïve, Charles. So naïve,' Dan said with a laugh. 'By the way, where did you get this yogurt? It's yum.'

'The supermarket.'

'Really! I haven't seen this brand before.'

'It's only in certain inner-city supermarkets.'

'It's really quite tasty,' he said.

'It's the extra cream that makes it so nice.'

'You don't mind if I take it. I want to look up the exact brand online.'

'You can take my bloody fridge, for all I care. Now, tell me why you're reading my texts?'

'All the chatter. Russian oligarchs funding literary magazines. Sam Woo. Kitty Wild … soon to be Roxanne Wild.'

'You've read the texts all wrong. Kitty Wild is a novelist, or at least that is her nom de plume. Her real name is Mary White, a seventy-year-old church-attending grandmother, writing her next erotic novel about a millionaire surgeon. As her hopeful publisher, I suggested she change the name and profession of her protagonist.'

'A grandmother writing erotic fiction? Don't make me laugh,' scoffed Special Agent Dan. 'You'll have a devil of a time explaining all this to the CIA.'

'What?'

'The CIA have asked us to question you, and one of your associates, Boris Petrović, about a possible Indonesian–Chinese invasion of the Top End. They want to know if it's linked to increased chatter online about a Chinese invasion of Taiwan.'

'This is out of control,' I said, shaking my head at the absurdity of it all. 'There are no Chinese agents infiltrating my magazine. There is no Indonesian–Chinese invasion of Australia—'

'It's the Russians then. Good,' said Dan. 'I can work a deal for us if it's the Russians. If it's the Chinese, then that'd be serious, but if it's the Russians, then there's money to be made.'

'Excuse me,' I said, shaking my head. Had I walked into the right apartment? Had I slipped into an alternative, absurdist fictional reality. Maybe Yamparti, Boris and Karen had really revolutionised western literature, and I was now in one of their absurdist stories … or worse still, I had walked into a Kafka novel. 'There are no Russian agents in *Imagine*,' I said.

'You visited St Petersburg just before the Ukraine war. Is that where the Russians acquired you?'

'How did you know I visited St Petersburg?'

'I told you, I'm from ASIO, and we know everything about everyone?' Now, I asked a simple question: is that where Russian intelligence acquired you?'

'No!'

'Then why did you take an office next door to a well-known front for Russia's foreign intelligence activity.'

'I only took the office because I liked the Spanish style of the building. It reminded me of my aunt Bella, who nearly modelled for Salvador Dali.'

'You're a fascist then.'

'No.'

'Look, Charles, work with me,' said Special Agent Dan, sighing. 'Have you heard of the Steele dossier?'

'No.'

'The CIA and their political paymasters are desperate for stories on nefarious Russian collusion with right-wing politicians and operatives. I know the names of several lawyers in the United States, connected to prominent US political actors, who will pay top dollar for a report about Russian infiltration into the media. We get them to leak it to the press. The media will salivate over this story. My god, the money I could get us for exclusive rights with a US cable news service. All we need to do is spin in an American angle. You don't know any US Republican politicians, by chance? Or better still, any right-wing media personalities, either here or in the United States.'

'No. Now, get out of my apartment before I call the cops.'

'Cops won't come.'

'Good, I can beat you to death with my Nimbus 2000, in peace,' I said, grabbing it again, and cocking it over my head.

Special Officer Dan sighed, and then he rose from the couch. 'You're making a big mistake. A big mistake, Charles. I know this is all some amateurish joke. But you'll have a devil of a time convincing the press this is one big prank gone wrong. A story of Russian interference in right-wing media is too alluring for them to give up. Narrative is king in media. Follow my strategy, and we can at least make a motza out of this, while the story still holds and before the press moves on to the next outrage.'

'Out!'

'Here's my card, if you ever change your mind,' said Dan, putting his business card on the coffee table.

'Get out!'

'Can I take the yogurt?'

'You can take the ruddy spoon too. Now get out, before you become the first Spook to be beaten with a quidditch stick.'

I followed special agent Dan as he walked to the door, my quidditch stick still loaded over my head, ready to fall on his head.

'You don't mind signing this form to say I was here on official business at this time.' Special Officer Dan took from his pocket a slip of paper. 'You don't know the devil of a time I have in claiming overtime and expenses in the federal public service. I've deducted for the yogurt—'

I stormed to the door and opened it. 'Out!'

'Thanks for the yogurt and the spoon—'

'Out!'

'If anyone calls, tell them I was here till ten. I get double time and a half, if I work past ten.'

I slammed the door shut on him.

CHAPTER 27

THE HONEY TRAP

'What have you done to me, Sam?' I cried, dropping the Nimbus 2000. 'This has got out of hand.'

'*Relax, Charlie boy.*'

'How can I relax. I have two spy agencies, the press and my nan believing crazy stories about me. All because of you.'

'*You have to laugh at the absurdity of it all,*' said Sam.

'God, what stories are they writing about me now?' I groaned, firing up the laptop, and sure enough, the top story in my news feed screamed: *Russian Spies infiltrate Right-Wing Media.*

Beneath the headline was my photo in a Victoria Grammar blazer, and next to this was my photoshopped picture of Kitty Wild.

'They have access to all my communications — texts, emails, even phone calls. Oh my god!' I blushed as I considered my Google searches for the last month.

The story from AAP read: *Australia's Security Intelligence Organisation is investigating a Russian honey trap operation targeting leading right-wing media figures.*

'*You have only published two editions, and already you're a leading right-wing media figure,*' said Sam. '*That was fast.*'

The article was vague and didn't mention me, only Sam and Pierre Bezuhov.

Another article appeared in my news feed, this time from *The Age* newspaper: *Ex-prime ministers call for Royal Commission into the Murdoch Press.*

The article began: *Two former prime ministers have issued a joint statement demanding the Federal Government call an urgent Royal Commission into the Murdoch Press. This follows disturbing claims of Russian meddling in a leading literary magazine and the spreading of hate speech …*

I didn't read any more of the self-indulgent twaddle and closed the web page. 'I'm not connected to the Murdoch Press,' I cried.

'Narrative, Charlie boy,' said Sam. *'Narrative. Journalists and politicians will twist any story no matter how obtuse, into their preferred narrative.'*

I flipped to the Melbourne *Herald Sun*.

Eugene had dug himself an even bigger hole for himself with his apology. Not only did no one in the Melbourne literary community believe him, he now inflamed the conservative blogosphere. Andrew Bolt wrote an entry on the saga. He even doubted the whole Russian infiltration story. His post received over two hundred comments.

The Daily Telegraph, in faraway Sydney, also carried the story. Tim Blair wrote a blog entry. I had to laugh at the savage and witty comments left on the post. As always, the conservative blogosphere saw the whole thing as a hoax before anyone else.

But now I realised Dan and Sam's point. It hit me like ice-cold water to the face. To the press, 'narrative' was king. As long as the story fitted one of their favoured storylines, the press wasn't going to let this story go anytime soon. For it had all the essential ingredients they loved: Russian femme fatales, Russian and Chinese spies, shadowy right-wing figures, private schoolboys gone wrong, plus the hint of sex. No matter how absurd it became, they would keep hammering this square peg of a story into their nice, rounded narratives.

I shivered, but Sam giggled. 'What is it, Sam?'

'*Poor Eugene,*' Sam replied with a smirk.

'I don't see anything funny in any of this, especially for me,' I said. 'I'm in a lot of trouble with a lot of people, especially my nan.'

But Sam laughed. '*You gotta love it, Charlie boy. What a difference a few words can make. With a few clicks of a mouse, Eugene has gone from being a daring, edgy, up-and-coming novelist, challenging the existing paradigms, to an immature, insensitive, racist, snooty, private schoolboy twerp, writing clichéd character stereotypes.*'

I may have gone on reading my news feed, except all my digital devices exploded: my mobile phone with text and voice messages — some from journalists wanting interviews or comments, some with death threats from people who knew where I lived, and the rest were just nasty comments.

My laptop also pinged with one new email after another from all manner of people, with many more death threats, and a plethora of obscenities.

It was when I switched off all my devices, the knocking on the front door began.

I froze, then jumping to my feet, I crept to the front door and looked through the peephole.

A woman, with a TV camera crew behind her, stood on my welcome mat.

'Mr Western. Mr Western. It's channel Nine. We have a few questions about Kitty Wild,' said the TV reporter, clearly sensing my presence on the other side of the door.

I tiptoed back to my bedroom and packed a few clothes, a toothbrush and brush, before placing the call through to Raj. 'Come get me,' I said, giving him the side street I lived on.

Then after ringing off, I took my bag, and locking the backdoor behind me, and with my knapsack slung over my shoulder, I quietly scaled the side fence and fell into the courtyard of my neighbour's unit. Tiptoeing across his concrete backyard to the opposite fence, I carefully scaled it, smiling at my cleverness, before jumping right into a nest of TV reporters having a coffee break.

CHAPTER 28

TV News

I shrieked as I hit the footpath, realising my leap had landed me in the nest of vipers I had tried to avoid. The blonde-headed TV reporter I landed next to screamed, jumping perceptibly on the spot, the boiling coffee she held splattering all over her bare arm.

The TV crews and I traded opened-mouthed looks before the lights clicked on, the cameramen aimed their equipment, and the reporters threw microphones under my mouth.

There was no point in running, so I shrank back as Sam stepped forward to my rescue.

'We are ready to take questions? Try your best? What narratives do you wish to spin tonight?'

'Mr Western, did you change the content of your magazine?'

'We changed the contents of the magazine but only to better reflect the intention of the authors. Isn't Israel the real victim in the Middle East?'

'Do you wish to apologise for the contents of your magazine?' another journalist asked.

'Will you apologise for your coverage?' Sam shot back.

'Is it true about Russian agents in your magazine?' another journalist asked.

'Where did you meet Kitty Wild?'

'Are you working with Russian intelligence?'

'Only one question at a time,' said Sam. 'Now, firstly about Kitty Wild. She is a talented author whose debut novel Write Creative Press has the honour of publishing later this year. *Whipped Cream* is the title, and it's about a spy by day, vampire by night. We will also be publishing another author called Boris Petrović. He wrote a novel called *Terror at the Airport*, which outlines a plot to take over Australia by foreign forces.'

Even as Sam said this, I saw the problem. I had secured Boris. Or Boris had no other options, at least. But Mary hadn't signed on the dotted line. I realised now that Sam was not only reckless but would lie all the time.

Sam, however, wasn't stopping now. He had clearly decided to give them what they wanted: a story to really hit the news. 'I've just been visited now by ASIO,' he told them.

A tremor of excitement ran through the assembled journalists.

'What did they want?' one asked.

'Charles' yoghurt.'

The press pack fell quiet. I could even hear the hum of traffic from St Kilda Road.

'Excuse me?' one of the journalists asked.

'They took Charles' yoghurt and spoon. I intend to sue ASIO on his behalf, for the full amount. He also wanted us to sign his overtime form.'

Even wincing under the glare of lights, I noted the journalist's eyes widen, the hamster wheels of their minds turning slowly, considering my last statement. In their rat-like brains, I imagined thoughts coalescing into a question, then into this either/or proposition. Were they speaking to the right person, or were they in fact speaking to a madman?

Luckily for me, or for them, Raj's car came around the corner and stopped in the middle of the street.

'Now, if you excuse us, we need to get Charles' spoon back.'

Before they could ask another question, Sam and I had stepped out into the street and jumped in the back seat of Raj's car.

'Drive,' I said to Raj.

'Where?'

'The nearest motel and make it quick.'

'Let me look one up on Google.'

'Drive!' I screamed.

'Like in the movies?' said Raj.

'Like in the movies!' I repeated as the journalists crowded around the car, like seagulls about an abandoned half-eaten meal of fish and chips.

Raj put his foot on the accelerator, and we sped away. Our sudden acceleration would make a perfect final shot for the camera crew, I thought. Already, I imagined the camera shot, with the voice over: 'Right-wing publisher makes his getaway, refusing to answer questions.'

'Will this be like the gangster movies, where we hold up in a motel room playing cards and eating takeaway food?' asked Raj. 'I see it all the time in the old American movies.'

'I do like the idea, but it won't be like that tonight.'

'I did drive for the mafia a few years ago,' advised Raj.

'It'll be nothing like that,' I said.

I made Raj zigzag through back streets. Raj might have driven for the mafia, but he wasn't too clever, for he drove back past the press pack now packing up, twice, before dropping me off at a motel two blocks from home.

I paid Raj for the fare, plus two hundred to remain on call, then settled down for the night under the name of Sam Samuel.

My motel room was a disaster, just like my situation. My mood reflected in its décor: drab and chaotic. An unclean stench of body odour hung to every surface of this claustrophobic and poky abode.

The sounds of TVs, a baby crying, and people talking in strange tongues permeated through the thin walls, along with the odour of takeaway curry. Outside, stilettos echoed on the concrete walkway, of the women of the night going to and from assignments. Somewhere, a drunk argued with the moon.

I dared not turn on the TV or fire up the laptop, lest I see mine and Sam's face plastered all over the news.

Instead, I paced the room, my mind spinning like a Catherine wheel powered by a cocaine-fuelled hamster, shooting off one vivid-coloured and paranoid thought after another. 'Thanks to you, Sam, I'm in a world of trouble,' I said, pointing into the vanity mirror.

'*But you have to admit this is fun,*' he said.

'Fun! Fun!' I cried.

'*Your name is in all the newspapers. You're famous.*'

'For all the wrong reasons!' I shouted.

Someone in the next room banged on the thin walls.

I continued pacing and arguing with Sam, in a lower tone.

'I need this to end. Tonight,' I said.

'*No.*'

'I need you to back down, Sam.'

'*Never. This is war.*'

'You're destroying my reputation.'

'*I'm making it,*' said Sam. '*I'm launching your career.*'

'You're destroying me. Have you seen the number of death threats I've received?'

'*Don't be such a nervous nelly,*' said Sam. '*I know how to handle this. Tomorrow, we go to the office and clear out all our things. I'll sack Karen, Boris and Yamparti, if they haven't already resigned. We then give up the lease in the office, before becoming a wandering nomad going from place to place, staying one step ahead of the mob, putting out the magazine solo. You'll be fine. You just need to trust me on this. I promise that tomorrow will be the dawn of a new life.*'

CHAPTER 29

THE MOLVANIANS

I slept little that night, tossing and turning, wondering what idiocy the next day would bring. By morning, I had over 300 voice messages and 2000 emails. I refused to listen to or look at any of them.

At dawn, I dressed unrefreshed, ordered room service, before setting off for the office, determined to let Sam lead the way.

I would try to pass unnoticed into the office, grab as much as I could before booking online a place to live. My strategy was to lay low and become a digital nomad, as Sam wanted.

I was thinking about my next move, whether I should be walking so conspicuously down St Kilda Road without a disguise, when a white eight-seater van came to a screeching halt beside me on the service lane, its side door thundering open.

'Western! Step into the van,' said a bald man with a gruff European accent.

I picked up my walking speed as two large men in suits jumped out of the van and came either side of me. Before I could protest or make a dash, a hand came from behind and placed a handkerchief over my face. With one sniff of the sharp acrid cloth, I lost consciousness.

I woke in the van coughing and spluttering, with two men staring at me on the opposite seats. The man nearest the window looked like Lenin, but with more good-natured eyes and a pointy white beard. The one next to him was bald and pudgy with a scar running from the top of his head to the corner of his left eye.

I blinked and coughed, taking several deep breaths. We moved slowly through the peak-hour traffic.

'I apologise for the interruption to your morning walk to work,' said the bald man with the scar. 'We promise this will be a short meeting.'

'Who are you and what do you want with me?' I asked, still blinking, not yet fully conscious.

'As to who we are, that unfortunately we cannot disclose. What we want from you is information.'

'I can give you a lot of that,' I said, 'though none of it would be interesting. Now, let me out.'

'We want to know about Dr Sidrov and his quantum entanglement bomb?' asked the man with the scar.

'Okay, listen, this has been a big misunderstanding. There is no quantum entanglement bomb.'

'Is he working for your country's defence industries?' enquired the bald man.

'No.'

'The Americans?'

'No.'

'The English?'

'No!' I shouted. 'You have this all wrong. There is no bomb. There is no Dr Sidrov. There is no plot to invade Australia by the Chinese and Indonesians.'

'An invasion? When?' said the bald man, wide-eyed and leaning forward.

'Holly molly! There is *no invasion*! There is *no* Dr Sidrov and *no* stupid quantum entanglement bomb. All of these are plot points in a stupid and badly written unpublished manuscript I had the stupidity to consider financing.'

'So, it is disinformation, then?'

'No!' I shouted. 'This has got out of hand. It's not part of any disinformation campaign by ASIO or any other foreign intelligence.'

The man who looked like Lenin, and who all this time eyed me closely, whispered something in a European tongue to the man with the scar. They talked animatedly for several minutes.

My head moved from one head to the next, like a spectator at the Australian Open, not understanding a word they spoke so passionately. 'I suppose you lot are Russian?' I asked.

The van stopped. The two men frowned. The atmosphere in the van tensed. Harsh foreign tongues came from other seats.

'So, if you're not Russians. Ukrainians, then?'

'No.'

More harsh words followed.

'Polish? Lithuanians?' I rattled off a few other European countries.

'For your safety, it's best you didn't know.'

'All right, be like that then, 'I said, crossing my arms. 'I'll call you Molvanians.' I chuckled at the remembrance of the mock travel guide to the fictitious East European Country called Molvania — a land untouched by modern dentistry, the front cover drooled, with a picture of a man without any teeth. I gave the book to my Nan two Christmases past, and we laughed our heads off for a good week as we took it in turns reading entries over several bottles of wine.

'We're not from there.' The man with the scar frowned.

Mr Lenin again said something to Scarface in his native language. Scarface answered, then turning to me, he said, 'We want you to come and work for us.'

'How can I work for you when you won't tell me what country you're from.'

'We are prepared to pay you big money, for you to be our cultural informant,' explained Scarface.

'We need to replace our current agent in this space,' continued Lenin. 'And with your close ties to up-and-coming cultural figures, you would be an invaluable acquisition.'

'I would hardly consider the people I know "up-and-coming or invaluable".'

'Oh.'

'Look, I don't know who you are, and frankly, after the last few days, I don't care. Just stick with your current agent?'

'We can't,' said Lenin.

'He's selling his Toorak hair salon and is retiring to the Gold Coast,' added Scarface.

'He was your country's hairdresser to the stars,' said Lenin. 'We got all the latest inside gossip on all your TV celebrities and social influencers.'

'What value would that have been?' I asked.

'It is important to know what is going on at the heart of your culture, and TV and social media seem to be important to your society,' said Scarface.

'Today, it is in your social media feed and on your TV,' said Lenin. 'Tomorrow, it is your country's reality.'

'Why don't you buy *New Idea*, or *Woman's Day* or any of the other gossip magazines? They'll give you all the information you need.'

'New idea?' said Scarface.

'Woman's day?' said Lenin, scratching his bald shiny head.

I wanted to slap my forehead at their stupidity. Instead, Sam rose to the surface, wanting to play.

'If you want to attract the right double agent in Australia, you first need to consider penalty rates,' said Sam. 'Have you consulted the Fair Work Commission for the appropriate award rate for double agents in Australia?'

The two men's eyes widened and their mouths fell ajar with clear incomprehension.

'Obviously, you haven't heard of nine-day fortnights, or penalty rates for public holidays. I know this wonderful ASIO agent who will give you all you want, as long as you pay him in creamy yogurt,' I said. I then realised, with annoyance, that Dan Oberon's business card remained on my coffee table.

'We would be most interested in acquiring this ASIO officer and you into our team.'

The van that had been travelling slowly stopped. Scarface leant over and slid open the van door with a *whoosh* to reveal the corner of Swanston Street and Flinders Lane.

'Well, Mr Western, this is where we must part.'

I stepped out, thankful to breathe the fresh cool air of late autumn Melbourne.

I took only a few steps when Scarface said, 'We will be in touch, Mr Western.'

'I hope not too soon,' I said before turning and continuing to walk away.

Scarface called out again, 'Western, be careful at the demonstration today.'

'Demonstration?' I asked, but the van door thundered closed, and it sped away, the cars it cut off beeping furiously.

CHAPTER 30

RICK

To calm my galloping heart, and steel myself for the office, I went to the Young and Jackson and ordered a double whiskey, which I downed before ordering another. While I waited, I contemplated the last words from my eastern European friends and wondered whether I really should go to the office after all.

'A bit early for a drink?' an American voice at my side said.

A middle-aged man in a blue tailored suit, with receding dark hair, and Italian sunglasses tucked in his top jacket pocket, who smelt of expensive aftershave, slid next to me and smiled.

'I suppose you're from the CIA?'

'We should talk, Charles. Or is it, Sam?'

'It depends on my mood,' I said, grabbing my newly made whiskey and taking a sip.

'Let's sit,' said the American.

'I don't normally drink with strangers.'

'Consider me a friend.'

'Tell me your name, at least.'

'For the purposes of this meeting, call me Rick.'

We took a seat in the deserted bar and stared into each other's eyes for a long time, like star-crossed lovers, Rick stirring his flat white.

'Do I get a prize if you blink first?' I asked.

'We want to know how you stumbled across our protocols for the data interchange model for security information management?'

'The protocols for data interchange model, excuse me … what?' I said, shaking my head at this mouthful of words.

'The data interchange model for security information management protocols.'

'I don't know anything about them.'

'Don't play dumb with me, Charles. Uncle Sam and its alliance partners have been working secretly on it for the last decade. Not a soul knows about them. We want to know how you came across them and who you work for?'

The look on my face clearly prompted Rick to peer over his shoulders, and seeing the room still empty, he leant across the table and enunciated each word slowly in a whisper, 'The data interchange model for security information management protocols. Or DIMSIM, for short.'

'DIMSIM? Oh …' I said as a little bell, like the St Kilda Road trams, tingled in my head.

'How did you find out about it and from whom?' asked Rick.

'You know that reading my text messages is illegal?'

'Everyone is reading everyone's correspondence, emails, texts, phone calls. Welcome to the twenty-first century, my friend.'

'You have read the text messages all wrong.'

'You wanted to pass it onto your operative Boris Petrović.'

'Operative?' I scoffed. 'Boris might be many things, but operative is not one of them.'

'We want to know who you're working for and what game you're playing?'

'I'm not working for anyone, and I'm not playing any game.'

'Don't toy with me, Charles. You're running a sophisticated operation, pretending to run a fictional magazine, all the while spying. I must say Boris' cover as a self-published author is convincing. We spent four hours last night interrogating him, and all we got was some story about a secret cabal of feminist lawyers and Mossad working together.'

'It's a convincing cover because it's true! Or at least in Boris' mind. He thinks he's an up-and-coming self-published author. And he's a very bad and annoying one at that. As for being a magazine publisher, has it ever occurred to you, I might be one and not involved in any espionage ring?' I shouted this, exasperated at Rick, the Molvanians, ASIO, the press, Nan. At everyone!

'Shh,' said Rick, looking over his shoulders. 'Keep your voice down.'

'I'm a publisher,' I hissed, leaning my head across the table.'

'No.' Rick laughed, shaking his head.

'Why?'

'Because it's too absurd. Here is this young man with a small fortune to his name. He could do anything he wants, yet he sets up a literary magazine in the middle of Melbourne. He employs a young left-wing editor, then in the second edition changes the editorial direction.'

'Sam wanted to teach her and a few others a lesson.'

'Sowing discourse. I thought that was your game. But who for?'

'No one! For goodness' sake. Isn't this small beer for the CIA,' I said, finally slapping the table in exasperation. 'Why aren't you in the Ukraine fighting the Russians, or focusing on the Middle East or watching the Chinese?'

Rick smiled and stirred his coffee. 'Your father took many trips to mainland China?'

'What are you suggesting?'

Rick took a sip of his coffee and considered me closely over the rim of his cup. 'You took a trip to China with your father also?'

'One trip, and I spent the whole time in the hotel in Hong Kong sick. Look, this has got out of hand. As I said, you're barking up the wrong tree. I'm not a Russian asset or a Chinese spy. I don't have any hidden agenda. I'm not trying to acquire talent or set up a spy ring. When I referred to "dim sim", I was referring to the Australian version of the dumpling, not some data interface whatchamacallit.'

'What's your game then?'

'How many times do I have to say this. I'm not running any game or playing any angles.'

'You mean to tell me you set up a literary magazine for the hell of it. Employed a lot of crazy people, then deliberately inflamed the left.'

'Self-sabotage, or that is what my therapist says I like to do.'

Rick laughed. 'I don't believe you.'

'It's true.'

'You did it deliberately?' said Rick, frowning, the penny it seemed finally dropping into the slot of his mind, and the song of truth beginning at last to play.

'Yes.'

The look of shock on Rick's face told me he now believed me. 'Then you're a fool. Do you know the left take no prisoners? They'll kill you, after of course they cancel you for life for mocking their "sacred cows". The Islamists have nothing on these people.'

'If they attack me, then I'll report them to the police.'

'The police won't do anything. They're as afraid of the left-wing mob as everyone else.' Rick looked around at the empty bar before leaning forward and whispering, 'If I was you, Charles ... or Sam ... or whoever you decide to call yourself today, I wouldn't go to your office after your drink. I would quit this city on the next train or flight. Get as far away from Melbourne as possible until people cool down.'

'No,' said Sam, rising to the occasion. 'Charles refuses to run away like a scared little boy. All his life he's run. Not now,' Sam said.

I was shocked at his bravery.

'At least I warned you,' Rick replied, shrugging his shoulders and rising to his feet.

'Rick,' I said. 'Can you tell the others in your intelligence community that this was one big prank.'

'Of course,' he confirmed with a smile. 'But don't think this is the end of your troubles, though.'

CHAPTER 31

THE DEMONSTRATION

After downing a third whiskey, I summoned enough Dutch courage to walk to the office. I didn't know what to expect or who would be lurking for me in the shadows as I exited the elevator. I half expected to be attacked as soon as I unlocked the door of the office. I even imperceptibly jumped in fright as a chair creaked in the darkness of the unlit room.

But instead of a fist from the corner, Karen snapped forward in her seat as I clicked on the light. From her unkempt hair, bleary eyes, and the rubbish bin overflowing with empty fast-food containers, it looked as if she had stayed all night in the office and had only drifted to sleep in the last hour.

'Waiting for Mr Prufrock to call?' I asked.

'Yes, and I hope it's soon.' She yawned. 'Barry has been calling me every hour wanting to know when I'm coming home. He thinks I'm having an affair. He thinks I'm having an affair with you.'

Great, I thought. Just what I needed. Add jealous husband to secret service agents, the press, Yamparti, Boris and Eugene. Not to mention whatever crazy person wanted a piece of me today. 'Look, about J. Alfred Prufrock,' I started.

'Before you say anything,' Karen said. 'Let me show you what I've been working on all night.'

I stood over Karen's shoulder as she showed me a possible change to the artwork for the magazine.

She had changed the font size, the coloured background, also the graphics. She had changed the mast head to a photo of the Princess Bridge at dawn, with the sun bursting through the buildings, bathing the bridge in a golden hue.

Seemingly noting my gaze, she explained, 'I went out and took a photo of it this morning ... I thought you might like it.'

'It's beautiful,' I said. 'You have an eye for photography.'

'I spent all predawn camped out waiting for the right light.'

'You should do all our photographs from now on. Maybe that is your true calling, not writing.'

'Thanks.' She sighed. 'You know I really don't think this writing business is all that it's cracked up to be. I've been thinking about giving it up.'

'Look ... about J. Alfred Prufrock——' I began.

'I know he's not real,' said Karen. 'In my heart, I realised it was all a prank even before Yamparti pointed it out.'

'Then why didn't you say anything?'

'Because sometimes it's better to believe in a falsehood than an ugly truth. Or worse, have no belief at all. It's the belief that's important, Charles, not the object. The feeling of euphoria I experienced after reading the letter from J. Alfred Prufrock makes up for the realisation it was a forgery. Does that make sense?'

Before I could say anything, a commotion in the street stole my attention. A hundred confused voices all mingling into one cacophony came from the street below, followed by the high-pitched squeal of electronics. I covered my ears.

Karen and I went to the window. A swarm of people spilled onto

Flinders Lane. Already a bank of trapped cars honked like geese, and a few motorists out of their cars tried to move people away, while police horses clomped into view.

'Fascism will never be tolerated in Australia ...' a loudspeaker voice cried. It was lost in the squeal of electronic distortion. A few in the crowd carried banners. One read: *Kill Fascist Right-Wing Pigs*. Another had a puppet of Rupert Murdoch, with a Hitler moustache, dangling from a noose and scaffold.

I wondered where they were marching to. Then with an involuntary shiver, as if an iced stalactite pierced my heart, I understood who their target was. Me!

From the corner of my eye, I noted the blood drain from Karen's face.

'Looks like the mob has come to lynch me.'

Outside, the chanting began ...

'No to the fascist press. No to the fascist press.'

The chorus of mindless voices droned louder and louder.

I took a deep breath as my whole body numbed.

'Looks like they've come for us,' said Karen.

'Someone needs to face them,' I said, taking from the coat rack, a heavy East German grey woollen overcoat I had bought at the Paris flea market, and then I headed for the door.

'Charles, you shouldn't go out there.'

'I'm not. Sam is.'

I opened the door.

'Sam?' said Karen.

Sam and I turned.

'Be careful out there,' she said.

'You should hide in the ladies down on the ground floor. Tell no one you work for *Imagine*.'

She nodded.

I descended the fire stairs slowly, taking one deep breath after another, Sam leading the way.

Sam and I stopped at the exit while I took one final big breath before opening the door and slipping unnoticed into the crowd thickening in the street.

The sound of chanting: 'Bring down the fascist press,' rang out over the clomping hooves of police horses, and the honking of car horns.

'Bring down the fascist press!'

Above, a TV chopper whirled.

'Excuse me,' I said to one person then the next, as Sam and I pressed our way into the crowd towards its buzzing centre. I, weak-kneed, wanted to turn around and run; Sam, confident, wanted to go to the heart of events and take control.

We reached the middle of the crowd, a small stand on wheels, surrounded by TV cameras and photographers and various scruffy people acting as officials. Sam jumped onto the stand, and before anyone could protest, he snatched the megaphone from a woman with purple- and yellow-streaked hair.

She gave me and Sam a withering glare before seeing my jacket and then clearly thinking of us as part of the program of speakers, stepping back to let Sam and me speak.

'I'm appalled by the fascism in this country,' cried Sam. His final words ending in a squeal of distortion. 'All about us are fascists,' he continued. 'Turn and look at the person next to you. What do you see? A fascist. When you wake up in the morning and look in the mirror? What do you see? A fascist.'

A few in the crowd looked oddly at Sam.

'What do we want?' said Sam through the megaphone. He lowered the megaphone and cupped his ear waiting for a response.

The sheep, however, looked at him, dumbly waiting for the answer.

He repeated through the megaphone, 'What do we want?' Then after a few seconds pause, Sam screamed into the megaphone, 'FASCISM!' A few seconds later, he added, 'When do we want it?'

'NOW!' the crowd chanted in answer.

The idiocy of the mob.

A few in the crowd squinted with recognition.

Someone grabbed at the megaphone.

'What do we want?' cried Sam.

'Fascism,' the crowd chanted back.

'When do we want it?'

'Now.'

How easy it was to train people to say and think the most ridiculous things. Men could become women, and women could become men, or global warming was a real and present danger, all through the act of chanting and repeating mindless slogans without critical thought.

Some in the crowd saw the danger. Several hands grabbed at the megaphone and my arm.

I shook them away.

'What do we want?' Sam chanted.

'Fascism,' the crowd chanted back.

'When do we want it?'

'Now.'

An unexpected punch to the back of the head pushed my lips into the megaphone.

'Help! Help! The forces of fascism are trying to silence me. Help ...'

These were the last words I remembered before the crowd erupted into screams and cries as Sam and I went under a crush of bodies.

CHAPTER 32

HOSPITAL STAY

It took a few minutes for the white ceiling to solidify before my eyes, and a few more minutes to register a steady *beep, beep* sound in my left ear, and a presence at my right.

'Charles, you're awake.'

I tried to turn, but my head exploded with pain, pinpricks of coloured lights popping like fireworks in my vision. I had an irresistible urge to vomit. The antiseptic disinfectant smell immediately took me back to my previous stay in the Royal Children's Hospital.

'Don't get up,' said Nan. 'I'll call the nurse.' Nan hit the button.

'What happened to me?' I asked, and almost immediately, a series of images flashed through my mind: Sam standing on the dais with the megaphone in hand; the wild faces of the crowd; the onrush of people towards Sam, then the blows.

'Those animals attacked you, Charles. The crowd stomped you underfoot as they turned on themselves. It took the riot squad two hours to stop the looting and violence.'

'My god,' I said, closing my eyes, trying to settle the throbbing in my head.

'I've told the police that my grandson had nothing to do with it. That you are a good boy. But they still want to speak to you. They want to know more about this Sam. Why he tried to inflame the crowd. Some want to charge him with inciting a riot.'

'Oh.'

'Charles,' said Nan, leaning into my view. She looked older, more worried than the last time I saw her. 'Who is Sam?'

'I told you … he's a friend.'

'Really?'

'Yes.'

'A few people are saying you're crazy,' she said. Her intelligent hazel eyes scanned my face. 'That Sam is a person you've made up. Tell me the truth, is Sam real? Have you been taking your medication?'

I opened my eyes, and concentrating on Nan's nose, I said, 'Sam is as real as you and me, Nan.' With that I closed my eyes, and only half listening to her onrush of words, I fell back into blissful unconsciousness.

I woke feeling better and brighter. Nan lay slumped in the armchair next to the bed, snoring, a strand of her perfectly coiffured hair loose and rising and falling with her breath.

A nurse came in. I immediately recognised her from my time in the Royal Children's Hospital when fighting leukemia.

'Cheryl. Remember me? Charles. Charles Western.'

'Of course, Charles,' she said, her face brightening. She came over and hugged me.

'I didn't believe it when I read the papers and heard you were back in hospital. The same good-natured and happy Charles Western from all those years ago. How brave you were. I can't believe how bad the crowd behaved, and the press saying you're some right-wing extremist.'

'I'm nothing of the sort.' I grinned.

'I never believe anything the press say. They always make things up.'

'You don't work at the Royal Children's Hospital anymore?'

'I do a few shifts if they ask me.' She smiled and looked at me closely. 'Remember all those stories you made up to keep the kids and the nurses entertained?'

'I do.'

'Remember the one story you made up when you heard about my breakup. How a daring fighter pilot would come to my rescue. Well, I ended up marrying a pilot from the Royal Australian Airforce. We now have two children.' She showed me the ring. 'It goes to show the power of stories, doesn't it. How you imagine things and they come true.'

'I'm happy for you, Cheryl,' I said.

Her eyes crinkled and studied me closely. 'Is this Sam one of your imaginary characters?' she asked. 'If so, he's a terrifying person to be around, organising riots and spy rings.'

'To deny Sam is to be Sam-phobic,' I said, my eyes now crinkling.

'Whatever the truth is, all the nurses loved you, Charles. You were always so sweet and kind.'

'Maybe too sweet and kind,' I suggested.

Nan stirred in her armchair.

'What day is it?' I whispered.

'Friday.'

'Friday!' I gasped. 'I've been out that long. What time is it?'

'Nine am.'

'Where are my clothes and mobile phone?'

'In the cupboard over there,' she said. 'What's special about today?'

'I'm meeting a girl tonight.'

'Oh, look at you Charles Western, all grown up,' said Cheryl. 'She is a lucky girl. Though I don't think the doctors will let you out tonight.'

'Of course.' My mouth curled up into another smile. 'I wouldn't dream of defying the doctor's orders.'

As soon as Cheryl left, Sam sprang from the bed, and tiptoeing over to the cupboard, he fished through my coat pockets. Finally, he pulled out the mobile and called. I, Charles Western, had no intention of defying the doctor's orders. Sam, however … well, that was a different story altogether.

CHAPTER 33

THE THIRD DATE

Hospital orderly Raj Katri, dressed in his white coat, arrived around 4pm for patient Charles Western.

'Where are you taking him?' asked Nan, rising from her seat.

'I'm … I'm …'

'He's taking me to get x-rayed,' I advised her.

'But the doctors didn't mention that to me,' said Nan.

'They just want to run a few more tests to be sure, Nan,' I said.

'I should call the nurses?' She reached for the call button.

'Don't, Nan, you wait there, I'll be back soon. This is all routine.'

'Yes, all routine,' said Raj in a deep voice.

Nan's gaze fell to Raj's Mickey Mouse socks protruding from beneath his jeans …

'I'm sure to be on video,' whispered Raj as we entered the busy hospital corridor, passing the armed guard stationed outside my door.

'I thought you said you drove for the mafia?'

'Yes, but only to take the boss' son to and from school.'

'Just wheel me to your car. And my name isn't Charles but Sam.'

'Okay, you're the boss.'

We got into Raj's car and set off for my flat.

'You know, Sam, you're famous.'

'Notorious,' Sam added.

'If this date doesn't work out, can I still introduce you to my sister Atfah? As I told you, she is studying medicine, and with your reputation and lifestyle, you're bound to need medical assistance.'

'Didn't we have this conversation last time? And wasn't she your cousin?'

'Did I say cousin? I'm sorry. She is my sister.'

'She comes ever closer to you by the day,' Sam said.

'Yes, and she is looking to stay permanently in Australia, and I thought with your standing in the community, you would be just the right type of gentleman to marry my cousin.'

'Sister.'

'Sorry, sister.'

'Sure, if this doesn't work out,' said Sam. 'I will marry Atfah.'

'It is a deal, Charles, I'm mean Sam,' said Raj, smiling.

Sam and I returned to a swastika painted on the door of my flat. On my welcome mat was an official-looking letter from a legal firm. I opened it. Eugene wanted to sue me. Sam threw that in the bin before moving inside.

We dressed in our best suit and spent a long time combing our hair in the mirror. I printed out the articles that mentioned Sam and me, then left the house.

'Western,' a voice shouted.

I spun around as Barry Tiven staggered into view from behind a plane tree, his fists raised.

'We need to have this out?' he slurred. 'Man to man.'

'Pardon?'

'What are you doing with my wife?' he slurred.

By the look of it, Barry had not only spent the day drinking, but several days passed out inside a whiskey vat. He reeked of it as he staggered unsteadily towards me.

'You've this all wrong, Barry.'

'I'm onto blokes like you,' he garbled, pointing his finger in my face. 'You reckon you're really special, with all your money and education, but I bet you haven't done an honest day's work in your life.'

I couldn't argue with that.

'You're pretending to be J. Alfred Prufrock. Isn't that right? Using her gullibility to get your way with her.'

'You must understand nothing is going on between us. Honestly.'

'J. Alfred Prufrock is a *fictional* character,' he now mumbled.

'You know that?' I said, genuinely shocked at his knowledge of early twentieth-century poetry.

'Fuck, everyone's read the poem at school. Even a plumber like me. Now, put your fists up.'

'I admit to writing the letter, but not to seduce your wife. I only did it as a prank.'

'So, you admit to leading her on.'

A group of people had gathered on the street to watch this, including a few photographers.

'Barry, we need to take this inside and discuss it over a cup of tea.'

'I don't want a fucken cup of tea. I want to take a swing at you.' He lunged, throwing his right fist in a haymaker at my head, but he stumbled as he did so.

I easily moved aside.

Luckily for Barry, Raj, out of the car, grabbed him as he fell to the ground, catching him before he dashed his head onto the concrete footpath. Cameras and mobile phones recorded the entire scene. Raj placed him on the nature strip, then we stepped passed him and rushed to Raj's car.

'Thanks for that,' I said as we buckled in.

'You're a dangerous man.' Raj laughed. 'I'm not sure whether I want you marrying my sister, now.'

'You can tell Atfah, drama and danger follow me wherever I go. But enough about your sister. I want you to stop the car,' said Sam, spying a florist.

Celeste's face on opening her door was one of surprise before it turned into a frown.

'What is it, Celeste?' Sam asked, peeking out between the three full-sized stuff bears we carried.

'Where am I going to put these?' she exclaimed before she came close. 'And who is this with you?' she whispered.

'Oh, this is Raj. He's our driver for this evening,' said Sam as Raj tottered through the door, weighed down by four baskets of roses he juggled in his arms, carrying one by the handle in his teeth.

After finding a cupboard to stuff the teddy bears and a clear table to place the baskets, we followed Raj back to his Uber.

'Did you say Raj is *our* driver for this evening?'

'All evening,' said Sam.

'Aren't the teddy bears, the roses, and a driver a little expensive?'

'One cannot put a price on love,' said Sam. 'Tonight, I'm taking you to the most expensive restaurant in all of Melbourne, the Vue de Monde on the 55th floor of the Rialto Tower.'

'I thought you hated heights?' said Celeste.

'Charles might, but not Sam. Sam isn't scared of anything or anyone.'

Celeste didn't laugh at the mention of Sam. Instead, she looked thoughtfully out the window of the car.

After seating Celeste, Sam ordered a bottle of the 1990 Veuve Clicquot Ponsardin La Grande Dame Reims.

'Charles, that is over a thousand dollars,' whispered Celeste, leaning across the table.

'I want this night to be special, Celeste. This may be our last time together.'

'Are you going away?'

'Have you been watching the news?'

'I don't watch TV or read the papers.'

'You didn't see or hear about the riot in the city the other day?' Sam asked, disappointed.

She shook her head.

'You're dating a dangerous man, Celeste. Many people are out to get me. See for yourself.' Sam handed over the printed copies of the various newspaper articles from the last few days.

As Celeste read these, Sam and I sat back and sipped the Veuve Clicquot and studied her wonderous eyes moving across the page.

'Is this true about the Russian oligarch, Pierre Bezuhov.'

'Of course not.' Sam chuckled. 'Pierre Bezuhov is a character from *War and Peace*.' Sam went on to explain the entire ruse. From pretending to be J. Alfred Prufrock, altering Eugene's manuscript, through to changing the second edition of *Imagine*. He punctuated his story with laughter at the idiocy of Karen and Boris, but Celeste remained unsmiling throughout. 'Why the long face?' Sam eventually asked.

'Why did you do that?'

'Do what?'

'Change their stories.'

'I wanted to teach them a lesson, Celeste. They talked about Charles behind his back and tried to humiliate him.'

'They humiliated you in private, so you humiliated them in public?'

'I wanted to teach them a lesson.'

'It seems so childish.'

'I did it to expose their hypocrisy.'

'You should show kindness to people, even to the people who do you wrong.'

'What, are you a Christian?'

'Yes. Religion is important to me,' she said, showing me her crucifix necklace. 'Forgiving people is important, Charles. Not only for the person who wronged you, but for your soul.'

'But they wanted to destroy Charles. All Charles' life, he's been turning the other cheek: humiliated and treated like a child. I'm only here to protect him.'

'You mistake protecting someone with inflicting harm on others. In your desire to punish wrongdoers, you have become the bully. You pretend to be Sam so you can be cruel and spiteful. These are the acts of a child. Sam is a child. A cruel and self-indulgent one at that.'

'Life is hard and cruel,' said Sam. He and I crossed our arms and leant back in our seat.

'That is not true,' said Celeste. 'Life is wonderful and mysterious.'

'I know it is,' said Sam. 'But as Charles' father said, sometimes you need to punch first before the other person punches you.'

'That is not true. You should always give kindness and kindness will be returned to you in the same measure. What you put out, you get back in equal measure.'

I reached out my hand, or was it Sam's, to Celeste's hand, but she withdrew it.

Sam sculled his glass and poured another. He started to top up Celeste's glass, but she stopped him.

'I don't like champagne,' she said.

'I ordered it for us.'

'You should have asked.'

Sam plopped the bottle on the table.

'I don't like this side of you, Charles. This talking in the third person.'

The waiter came to our table, but Sam waved him away with a

dismissive flick of his hand.

We sat for a good minute in silence.

Finally, Celeste spoke. 'At first, I thought Sam was an amusing little idiosyncrasy. A way of expressing another side of yourself, Charles. One that had been buried down for so long. But not anymore. Sam is a cruel, vain and selfish creature, more interested in seeking vengeance than seeking to protect and guide.'

Celeste studied me closely with her expressive eyes, then added, 'I don't think you are well, Charles.'

'I'm fine.'

'Then you need to make a decision, whether to carry on with this childish Sam nonsense, or spend time with me.' Celeste rose to her feet.

'What are you doing?'

'I'm leaving you with Sam.'

'But why?'

'I wanted to have dinner with Charles. He's sweet, even if he is a little clumsy. He's afraid of heights but would take me for walks along the beach and buy fish and chips. But with Sam, everything is over the top: oversized teddy bears and thousand-dollar champagne. You need to decide who you are.' She then turned and left the restaurant.

I remained a few discreet minutes more, then paying for the champagne, I slunk from the restaurant, red-faced and bowed, sensing many eyes watching me leave. I descended to the carpark feeling as if my own heart plummeted with it, but whereas the lift stopped at level B2, my heart kept on going and going, crushing into a graphite pulp at the earth's core.

'That was a quick meal,' said Raj, sitting on the bonnet of his car, consulting his mobile phone. He looked around puzzled. 'Where is your date?'

'We had a fight.'

'Ah,' said Raj, opening the back passenger side door.

'Do you want me to introduce you to my sister?'

'No thanks.'

'Then let me take you to the night clubs. I know many where all the women are beauties like your date, and also very, very friendly.'

'No thanks, Raj. Can you just drive?'

'Where?'

'Anywhere.'

'Did I tell you I drove for the mafia when I first came to Melbourne.'

'Yes, you've mentioned it,' I said. 'You drove the big boss' son to school, I believe.'

'Ah yes, I did say that. But I also drove the bosses and his associates to all the night spots. If you like, I can take you to one of the best hotspots in Melbourne, which isn't written about in any guidebook.'

I turned my head and looked out the window.

Raj dropped the subject.

We travelled for a while in silence. I, looking out the window and feeling as miserable as the landscape we passed.

'Have you ever thought of an arranged marriage, Sam?'

'My name is Charles, not Sam.'

'Sorry, I thought you said your name was Sam.'

'My name is Charles. Sam is dead.'

Raj gave a forced laugh before saying, 'Have you thought of an arranged marriage, Charles?'

'No.'

'It is a better option. Look at the divorce rates in Australia. Look at all the time taken finding a partner, all the heartache and false trails. Going to nightclubs, or bars, or getting on the internet, and all you get is rejection after rejection. My marriage was arranged. My parents got together with my wife Lakshmi's parents and brokered a deal. We were married a year later and now have two sons and not a bad word between us in the last five years. Your parents know more about you and what will make you happy, than you do.'

'Both my parents are dead.'

'Oh, I'm sorry, Charles. Truly, I didn't know.'

'I do have a nan,' I said as a way of consolation. 'And she is always trying to matchmake me to one girl or another. If she had her way, I'd be married to one of her friends' granddaughters by now.'

'And what is wrong with that?' asked Raj.

'I want to choose the girl. I want to do something for myself. Nan is always trying to run my life. People are always telling me what to do.'

'If you do change your mind on the arranged marriage, I'm happy to broker a deal with Atfah.'

Raj said more, but I tuned out, turning my head to look out at the darkened and wet landscape. I didn't want to talk. I didn't want Raj providing advice like all the other people had done in the past. I wanted to be alone with my thoughts and feel as miserable as the night now awash with rain.

What was I doing? What was I thinking? Celeste was right. I was immature. A pathetic, privileged private schoolboy playing juvenile pranks on other immature and privileged people. I responded to the private cruelty of Yamparti, Boris and Karen with a public humiliation.

All my life, I had searched for love and approval, trying to buy affection by showering money left, right and centre. But people only came to me because of my money.

What was I trying to do with my life? Why did I start the magazine? Why had I employed people I despised? I knew the answers as soon as I asked the questions. Because they stroked my vanity. They told me what I wanted to hear, but which they personally didn't believe. Raj only liked me because I paid his fare at triple the rate. If I didn't pay him, he would drop me on a deserted road and drive off without a second thought.

Sam had tried to protect me from these people, but in doing so, he had only driven me further from those who mattered most. I was using

Sam to settle old schoolboy hurts and humiliation, but in doing so, I hurt the people I loved.

What was I to do? What was I to do?

I sighed. Time to call it a night. 'Raj, drive me back home.'

'Okay.'

'Also, how much do I owe you for the night?'

'You don't owe me anything.'

'Sorry?'

'Tonight, I drive you free of charge.'

'I don't understand?'

'After the way you've been treated by all those university students and how the newspapers lied about you, driving you is the least I can do.'

'I don't know what to say?'

'Be yourself and stay true to your mission. That is all anyone asks of you.'

'Raj, my new friend, take me to the city.'

CHAPTER 34

LETTER TO THE WORLD

After Raj dropped me outside the State Library, I booked a free computer and logged into my accounts. Raj was right, I needed to be true to myself. And to be true to myself, I needed to make a clean break, set the record straight, and make my confession. Only then could I start again on my one true path.

I wrote the following:

To the readers of *Imagine*, the press and the intelligence services on three continents.

I apologise unreservedly for misleading you.Let me begin by admitting what I did.

I changed the *Dreamtime in Suburbia* manuscript by replacing proper nouns such as 'Christianity' with 'Islam', and 'Jesus' with 'Mohammed'.

To Eugene Whiteford, I apologise unreservedly. You didn't deserve to be outed as Ki Goonawanda or have your manuscript changed.

Yamparti Jones, you were correct. I changed your essays by replacing the word 'man' for 'woman', and 'Palestinian' for 'Israeli'. I also added a lot of nonsense about women writers below your by-line. I apologise unreservedly.

To all the women writers, you're really good. Honestly. I only did it to stir things up, knowing a tiny minority of you don't have a sense of humour.

To Karen Tiven, I played a silly trick on you. I wrote a letter from J. Alfred Prufrock, the main character in a T.S. Eliot poem. I'm sorry you thought Prufrock a real person and, under his instructions, sent the changed manuscript of *Dreamtime in Suburbia* to the Carlton Mosque. That was a mean thing to do.

To the Islamic community. I hope we can still be friends.

To the Australian press, please note the following, in no particular   order.

There is no Russian spy ring.

There is no Chinese agent called Sam Woo.

Pierre Bezuhov is a character from *War and Peace*.

Kitty Wild is the pen name for a talented writer called Mary White, and I don't know any right-wing media personalities.

Sorry to ruin all your narratives. I hope you can forgive me.

What is my excuse for misleading you all?

I could say I did it to show how intolerant and racist most progressive politics is. How eager people are to believe stories that fit their narratives.

However, this would be a lie.

I didn't expect all of this to get out of hand as it did. I really did it because I wanted to strike back at those people who mocked my writing. I wanted to humiliate people I believed had treated me badly.

I paid private hurts with public humiliation.

I now wish to apologise for all those who fell for my thoughtless scam.

Yours sincerely,
Charles Western

After completing this letter and publishing it on the website and all social media accounts, I drafted an email to Celeste.

Dear Celeste,

I want to tell you how sorry I am. You're right, I acted like a silly schoolboy. A jerk, really. I feel so ashamed of my actions. I would change anything in my world to keep you in my life. I've told Sam to leave. He's gone.

Ever since I first cast eyes on you in the library, I've only wanted to be with you.

I would give up everything in my world, the magazine, my wealth, any part of my personality, so long as I could be with you.

I've written a retraction in my magazine and on the website.

I don't want this notoriety. I want a life with simple pleasures too, such as walking on the beach, reading good books, gardening, and laughter. A world filled with children and picnics and days driving through the countryside on warm spring days.

It's a world I want to share with you, Celeste.

P.S. I don't like champagne either.

Also, here is the recipe for 'dim sims' I found on Google:

Minced meat, cabbage, and seasoning, encased in a wrapper like that of a traditional shumai dumpling. They are typically rectangular, or sometimes a larger circular shape. They can be served deep fried or steamed and are commonly dressed or dipped in soy sauce.

After sending the email, I closed the computer and took a deep breath.

I knew it would only be a few minutes now. The state and big tech track our every move, monitoring and categorising every citizen's digital footprint.

I knew within seconds of opening my email that they would have tracked me to the State Library, but I didn't care. What was the point of running? This was the new world order now. Where psychopaths and narcissists controlled all the big institutions. And with the help of big tech, the deep state, and the media, they maintained their power through the control of information, destruction of reputation online, and soon they would be using the thin excuse of social credit to seize their enemies' bank accounts.

I wasn't prepared to fight them.

Sam might have, but he had gone. I wanted love, not to become a soldier in a never-ending war.

I sighed and rose to my feet and headed out the door. As expected, the steps of the library were forming with press and police.

I winced under the camera lights as they switched on, and the authorities converged.

CHAPTER 35

MOTHER'S DAY

Mother's Day — one of the saddest and most poignant days on my calendar. As per our custom, Nan and I took the 48 tram the two stops to Boroondara Cemetery.

There, we walked to Mum's final resting spot and placed, as per our annual ritual, a single white rose at her headstone. We then remained in silence for several minutes, listening to the wind whistling through the trees. Neither of us spoke as we considered her sacrifice and her many possibilities cut so short. This year it was my turn to say a few words. Nan and I had discussed the broad outline of this year's eulogy the night before.

Nan nodded for me to begin.

Taking a deep breath and with a trembling hand, I took from my breast pocket the notes I had spent all night writing and rewriting, a sense of impending betrayal sweeping over me. I took another deep breath, then stealing myself, said, 'Mum, thank you for your sacrifice. Thank you for giving me life. I know you were also an only child, so I realise how difficult it must be for my nan too on this day.'

Nan sobbed, but I didn't turn or place my hand on her back to comfort her this year. Sometimes to be kind, you need to be cruel.

'Last night, I came upon this poem by Victorian poet Christina Rossetti. I believe you would recite this to me now:

When I am dead, my dearest,
Sing no sad songs for me;
Plant thou no
roses at my head,
Nor shady cypress tree:
Be the green grass above me
With showers and dewdrops wet;
And if thou wilt, remember,
And if thou wilt, forget.

I shall not see the shadows,
I shall not feel the rain;
I shall not hear the nightingale
Sing on, as if in pain:
And dreaming through the twilight
That doth not rise nor set,
Haply I may remember,
And haply may forget.

This will be my last time visiting you in the cemetery, Mum.'

Nan inhaled sharply. From the corner of my eye, she stiffened straight. She turned to stare at me. I didn't respond. From the corner of the other eye, a shape emerged onto the path and came towards us.

'You may have died an earthly death, Mum,' I continued, looking straight ahead, 'but you continue to live on through the agency of God Almighty who made you, and the mercy of Christ who saved you.' I made the sign of the cross then let my hand fall to my side as Celeste took my right hand. Immediately, I felt the warmth of her touch enveloping my fingers, my palm, her life spreading up my arm to my heart.

'I can't believe you won't be visiting your mother, anymore,' sobbed Nan.

'Mum wouldn't want me to wallow in her death. She'd want me out in the world living and experiencing all that life has to offer. To honour her sacrifice, that's what I will do. I'll begin to live my life.'

Nan turned to face me, and she finally noted Celeste at my other side holding my hand.

'Nan, I would like to introduce you to Celeste. Celeste, this is my nan.'

Celeste smiled and bowed her head imperceptibly.

Nan's eyes squinted as she sized up Celeste.

'Nan, you may have lost a daughter, but with Celeste, you are gaining a grand daughter-in-law.'

Nan frowned, then her forehead creased with incomprehension. 'Excuse me, what?' she said.

'Nan, Celeste and I are engaged.'

I caught Nan just before she could fall onto the grave and knock her head on the headstone. I held her a long time, while Celeste looked inside her handbag for something to fan her with.

CHAPTER 36

A New Beginning

It made no sense to marry so quickly. 'You should wait and see whether your feelings are true,' they said.

However, we didn't listen or wait.

We married in a registry, Raj and Atfah as witnesses. After bringing Celeste's relatives out from France, we married again in front of everyone at St Paul's in the city, Raj as my best man, Celeste driven to the church in a horse-drawn carriage, society columnists splashing our big day in the papers.

We have moved to a small place by the beach in St Kilda and eat fish and chips near the water every Saturday night.

I still publish a magazine, but under a different name and format. I employ Karen Tiven to take photographs around the city. She has an eye for the unusual, the quirky. A homeless man slumped in the street, or the way the sun hit the faēade of one of Melbourne's many sumptuous goldrush-era buildings. Celeste and I create words for Karen's images. Sometimes a poem, or a short story. At other times, an inspired meditation on the human spirit. Our goal is always to produce something beautiful — words to inspire.

In the magazine, we include an interview with some random person from the street, accompanied by their photo. Karen does the interviews. We receive many favourable letters about these. We don't make money from the magazine, as yet. It is a labour of love. Something we create between our studies: Celeste with her psychology degree, and me with my business and commerce masters.

My aim in the short-term is to become a micro-investor, taking a small idea, or a small business and helping it grow, like I am doing with Kitty Wild's book, *The Sorcerer's Slave*, now one of the hottest sellers on Amazon.

I want to help people do what I tried to do with *Imagine*, but this time with guidance and structure I lacked, and didn't want. I've invited Terry Smith as a partner on my business venture: Write Creative Press.

I see Eugene occasionally in the city with his briefcase. I hear he went back to being an intellectual property lawyer. He dropped his lawsuit. The ridicule of being exposed as Ki Goonawanda and the blowback proved too much.

Occasionally, the second edition of *Imagine* and Eugene's book is mentioned with Ern Malley, and *The Hand that Signed the Paper* by Helen Demidenko, as one of the biggest literary scandals of the last one hundred years in Australia. I don't know why.

I never saw Yamparti again. She disappeared into the obscurity of the university system — no doubt in the tenth year of some three-year course.

I still see Boris occasionally in the papers or on *A Current Affair* as spokesperson for DADLAW. He seems happy enough. I don't know whether he still writes. I hope for his sake and the world he doesn't.

In my new life, I've forsaken alcohol, and I meditate daily. I also see Dr Regi on a regular basis and take all my pills.

Yet … Sam sometimes still speaks to me, usually in my dreams, or as I write. I don't tell Celeste or Nan of this. Instead, it is a secret between Sam and me. Of course, I am careful to keep him on a tight leash.

'If you have no talent or skill in your chosen field, Charles,' he sometimes

whispers to me as I daydream on the balcony of our new apartment, '*then there is only one thing left for you to do. Be as outrageous and disagreeable as possible. And as for the meaning of life … If you must hanker for one, then let it be the continuous striving towards some unattainable goal. And about daydreaming: never ever do it. Instead, live inside your dreams and only consider reality in the safety of your imaginative wanderings.*

'*If you follow these rules, Charles, you have the potential to go far. I have mapped out your daily routine; but let me compliment you first on your new life with Celeste. From where I sit on the balcony, I can see all the way to the Heads with the telescope. It's lovely here: the birds in the trees, the sound of the street below, and the tapping from your computer. That is what I want to hear from now on. The sound of you working away on your writing in the early hours. Don't worry if you think it is no good, just spend the morning putting it on paper. You have the rest of the afternoon for study, for your new business ventures and time with Celeste.*

'*Look at that world! Big, bright, inviting! Yes, Charles, the day is yours to do what you want. Maybe catch a tram into the city and take Celeste to the pictures. Or maybe you could stroll down Collins Street, arm in arm stopping at a café to watch the world pass you by, drinking down her accent, her scent, her beauty. Life is so much richer and wonderful when you are in love.*

'*I have placed your name with a local writer's group. I know you would be too shy to do so yourself, so I took your credit card and did the deed myself. I've also selected a leather jacket for you to wear at their meetings.*

'*I have another idea for your consideration. We rise early one morning and ascend in a hot air balloon with five thousand copies of the second edition of* Imagine. *As we reach the peak of our assent, we release them to the wind.*

'*Can you see it in your imagination, Charles? Copies of* Imagine *falling upon the city like snow. The people looking up from their commute to work as they wait at their bus stop, or their railway stations. Or as they walk down Lygon Street, Little Collins Street, or Acland Street and your magazine tumbles into their hands. Yes, Charles, the thing you love doing, your ideas and words falling from the sky, like manna from heaven. Imagine that …'*

AUTHOR'S NOTE

Thank you for reading *My Friend Sam*.

Please leave an appraisal of this novel on Amazon or at: www.writecreativepress.com/contact. All comments good, bad, and indifferent go a long way in helping the author.

You can contact the author directly by leaving a comment at: henrytlarsen@outlook.com.

For more details on upcoming books by this author, please visit: www.writecreativepress.com